"You're my best shot now, Kaylee. I don't know what else to do. I've prayed about it constantly."

"Yes, well, that may be okay for finding a bit of temporary peace, but you have to be proactive."

Eli frowned. "Why do you say that?"

"God helps those who help themselves. He's not going to do anything unless you start it, so you better come up with a plan."

"Is that what you've been taught? God isn't some passive overseer. He's powerful, strong, willing to do anything to bring back his lost sheep."

BARBARA PHINNEY

was born in England and raised in Canada. She has traveled throughout her life, loving to explore the various countries and cultures of the world. After she retired from the Canadian Armed Forces, Barbara turned her hand to romance writing. The thrill of adventure and the love of happy endings, coupled with a too-active imagination, have merged to help her create this book and other wonderful stories. Barbara spends her days writing, building her dream home with her husband and enjoying their fast-growing children.

Desperate Rescue

Barbara Phinney

Published by Steeple Hill Books™

STEEPLE HILL BOOKS

ISBN-13: 978-0-373-44260-7
ISBN-10: 0-373-44260-2

DESPERATE RESCUE

This edition published by arrangement with Steeple Hill Books.

www.SteepleHill.com

Printed in U.S.A.

But you brought my life up from the pit,
O Lord my God. When my life was ebbing away,
I remembered you, Lord, and my prayer rose
to you, to your holy temple.

—*Jonah* 2:6–7

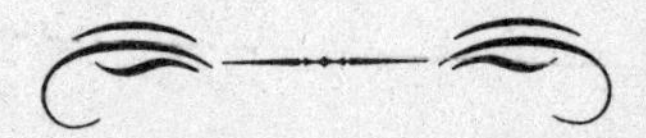

To my husband, my daughter and my son.

We grow in faith together, and I will always thank our Lord for each of you.

You make my life special and blessed.

ONE

Fear had a way of heightening the senses.

A chill crawled down Kaylee Campbell's spine as she neared the driveway of her rented home. Not from the cool autumn morning. No, this ominous shiver came from a foreboding sense of danger acquired after years of being watched and followed every waking moment.

Kaylee glanced around the quiet cul-de-sac in the central New Brunswick village chosen for its peace and security. It was too quiet.

Someone was watching her.

"Don't worry," she muttered, drawing in a deep, slow breath the way the counselor had taught her. "Go home. You're safe. You're free."

Her Saturday-morning walk had failed to soothe her nerves and neither did these words. Her chest tightened.

A car inched along the adjacent street. Over her shoulder she caught a glimpse of an out-of-province license plate.

The chilling wash returned. Her senses heightened; awareness ripped into high gear.

The car turned down her street. She listened a moment, then threw another glance over her shoulder.

Blond hair. A sinister sense of familiarity. Her heartbeat accelerated and she stopped with the pretense of tying her shoelace to cast a desperate glance around. Maybe one of her elderly neighbors was out this early.

No one. The cold autumn wind rattled the dead beech leaves that clung stubbornly to the tree on her front lawn.

Lord, help me. Keep me safe.

Doubt trickled into her as she tried the prayer. It wouldn't help. None of her prayers were heeded. Why should they be, after what she'd done?

She straightened, desperate to control the wild panic now racing through her like a torrent of spring rains.

Build a hedge of protection around me, Lord.

Nothing. She felt no safer now than a moment ago. And the car behind her was inching closer.

She pulled her control in sharply. Her fear was ridiculous. The nightmare of these past two years was over. There was not going to be the final confrontation Noah Nash had threatened.

She shut her eyes, screwing up the courage to take flight and race those last few yards to her house.

But her feet froze to the sidewalk beneath her. Her legs, stiff and beginning to ache, refused to obey.

She dared another peek over her shoulder. The car slowed behind her. It stopped. Its door opened. She gasped the choking kind of breath that seemed to lodge in her throat.

Noah Nash *had* come after her, just as he'd threatened.

In front of her and deadly close, stood the man she most feared and dreaded.

He'd come back to kill her.

Her world dissolved into darkness as her stiff legs melted to jelly.

Eli Nash let out a frustrated noise as he rushed toward Kaylee. This was his own fault. He'd been warned not to approach her. Even his own mother had firmly condemned his plan.

"You look too much like Noah. You two could have been twins," she'd said. "And you act too much like him, too. You'll end up scaring her half to death."

Shoving aside the warning, he caught Kaylee before she crumpled to the sidewalk. She slumped against him and he shifted to support her head as it rolled back. The boneless feel of her body surprised him as he dropped to his knees. Her jaw slackened and he heard a soft breath escape.

He wanted to kick himself for his own impetuous stupidity in not calling first, but there would be time to berate himself for that later. Right now, the best thing would be for him to simply carry her to her house and set her on her front lawn until she revived.

He knew he should have waited, but it was too late now, he thought as he lifted her off the ground. He should have used the police as an intermediary. Or a local pastor. Riverline had a church.

But he couldn't wait. Waiting could lead to more deaths, possibly even his own sister's.

Noah wouldn't think twice about killing a blood relative if it meant furthering his own plans.

A breeze drifted by, cool and sharp with the tang of autumn. In his arms, Kaylee Campbell shivered and awoke.

He peered down at her grimly, resisting the urge to sweep away the waves of black hair that fell across her cheek as her dark eyes fluttered open. Her skin looked so pale. Naturally pale, he hoped, not pale because the blood had drained from her delicate features at the sight of him.

She was lighter than she looked, not surprisingly. Noah had a habit of keeping tight control on his cult members, both the willing, such as his sister, and the unwilling, such as Kaylee, through malnourishment. It looked as if Kaylee hadn't yet regained her strength and weight.

"It's okay. You fainted."

Her eyes widened. Eli tightened his jaw. He was scaring the daylights out of her, but if he set her down she'd probably collapse again.

"I won't hurt you," he told her softly as he walked. "Let me carry you to your house. Where are your keys?"

She threw a furtive glance down at her right jacket pocket and her right hand moved ever so slightly. But she didn't offer them.

He considered helping himself to the keys, but any search, however modest, would scare her further. Instead, he leaned forward and set her down on her single, pitted cement step, waiting for her to produce her keys.

Keys in hand, she swiftly slid toward the door and

he knew he had to say something fast or risk losing the chance to explain.

Too late. No sooner had he stepped closer when her leg swung up and her foot connected with his midriff in one nasty, fluid kick.

He toppled to the lawn.

Stunned for a moment, he watched as Kaylee scrambled to her feet, tore inside her house and locked her door.

Then he sagged. Oh, this was just great. Well, he was bringing this all on himself, so he better learn a bit of patience. But after years of searching for his sister, he was desperate.

With a grimace of pain, he stood and rubbed his stomach. Through the door's small window Kaylee stared at him, wide-eyed. The expression wrenched his heart.

She was terrified. So scared she didn't realize that she'd dropped her house keys. His mouth a thin line, his brows lifted, he scooped up the keys and dangled them from his fingers.

"Ms. Campbell. Kaylee. I'm not who you think I am."

Her gaze darted around. Obviously, she was searching for some other way to defend herself, should he unlock her door. He had no intentions of doing that.

"I'm not Noah. Kaylee, listen! I'm his brother, Eli. Listen to me, please."

She snapped her head to the front, enough for him to catch the shock.

Patience. *Father, please help me. If You want me to be patient, help me now.*

Maybe he should be praying for his sister's life, instead. If she heard his prayer, she'd accuse him of being selfish, jealous, looking again to upstage Noah.

He took a step back. "Look at me. You can see I'm not Noah."

Kaylee shook her head. "No, I can't. You kept yourself hidden most of the time. You've cut your hair and shaved that beard. You won't get away with kidnapping me. I won't cooperate, Noah! There's nothing to hold me there anymore, thanks to you! You didn't fool me with Trisha's death. I know you killed her!"

She drew in a shaky breath and battled on, "I won't be blackmailed! You can kill the lot of those fools who follow you. I refuse to care!"

"Listen!"

"No! You threatened to kill me before, but you won't get away with it this time!" She turned to move away from the door.

He raced to the door. "Wait! I'm not going to hurt you! Just listen! I only want to talk to you."

Thankfully, she stopped. He fished his wallet out of his pocket. Then, from the battered slice of leather, he drew his driver's license.

He plastered it on the windowpane. "Who's this?"

She read it quickly but shook her head. "IDs can be forged."

With a growl, he thrust it back into his pocket. Thinking a moment, he pushed his short hair away from his hairline and tilted his face to the ground, showing her a scar. "Does Noah have this?"

She fell silent. *Thank You.* He'd finally reached her.

A brittle moment later, she answered, "Noah didn't cut his hair, so we didn't see his forehead. He kept hidden, too, and when we did see him, the room was always half dark."

Eli offered his left hand and the scattered islands of wrinkled skin, the remains of an old burn from when he and Noah had been playing with the woodstove at their grandmother's house, thirty years ago. "What about this?"

"I didn't see his hands, either."

Great. Back to square one. Just as he was trying to remember another childhood injury, she added with a soft whisper, "But you're left-handed. Noah's right-handed."

Of course. Relief sluiced through him and he let out a long sigh. "I forgot about that."

She met his stare, her expression soft as a deer's, with watery eyes shimmering. She wet her lips. "Who did you say you were?"

"Eli, his brother." He backed away from the door but she just stood there, staring at him, keeping the door firmly shut. "I need to talk to you."

"You want to talk? Talk. This is the only way we're going to communicate."

He sighed. Better than nothing. "I need you," he repeated. "You're the only one who can help me."

Kaylee blinked. So much had happened so quickly. This morning, she awoke and looked forward to her walk, anxious to put together her life after Trisha's...

After all the awful things that had happened...and all the things she'd done.

"Kaylee? Will you listen to me? I need your help."

Noah never begged. He had complete control over his followers.

Eli's voice filtered in through the myriad images that always surrounded Kaylee's thoughts of the cult. The compound, called The Farm by cult members, whisked through her brain. The gnawing hunger, the biting cold.

The tears at night, her sister begging for her compliance. At first. Then later, when she weakened—

Forget all that. "What do you want?"

He ran his fingers through his short hair, allowing her to study his face. Though she hadn't seen much of Noah, she'd seen his sharp blue eyes enough times, and the piercing stare always unnerved her. Eli's eyes were different. Softer.

Finally, he spoke. "My sister, Phoebe, lives with Noah. I need you to go back—"

"No!" Still focusing on Eli's face, she shook her head. "Forget it! You don't know what you're asking. I'm never going back there!"

He captured her gaze and held it. His tanned face wore a driven and determined expression. "You're the only one who can help me reach Phoebe. She won't talk to me."

"Then get your mother to. Everyone listens to their mother."

"My mother has tried, but each time she's written, the letters have been returned unopened. Both of my parents are getting old and can't travel. Mom tried to call, when they had a phone, but she was always told Phoebe was busy or that Noah would take the message."

That sounded about right. Noah owned a cell phone, but the few times it rang, only John or one of the men were allowed to answer it. She could still recall the one time it rang and there were no men. The women let it ring on and on, a creepy nonaction that still irritated her.

"We've all tried. I'm hoping that she'll at least talk to another woman who lived with her. Can you go back—"

Her breath clouded the cool pane of glass between them, thankfully breaking the lock his stare had on her. "Are you nuts? We can't help them! And I won't go back to try. Phoebe knows I hated all of them." She let out an incredulous laugh. "Trust me, you can't help them. I spent two years there! They're all beyond help."

Eli bent closer to the door. His pale brows pressed together. "Did you say that when you went looking to save your sister? Did you believe that when you went searching for Noah's compound? Remember how you got that info?"

She shrank away. "How do you know that?"

"You were on CNN, Kaylee. You paid a local to reveal the exact location of the compound."

He'd done his homework. Yes, she'd paid for the information. More than five thousand dollars. But she'd been desperate to find her sister, willing to deplete her meager savings. And she'd found out where exactly in eastern Maine they were.

Like Eli was now, she'd been anxious, hurt by her sister's actions.

She threw off the sympathy. "So why don't *you* just go talk to Phoebe? You're her brother, just as much as Noah is. Surely she'd see you? Can't you say that your parents are worried about her, too?"

His nod of agreement was barely perceptible. "Yes, they are concerned. And at a loss of what to do. Phoebe had just turned eighteen when she left and they couldn't force her to come back. But she was so innocent."

Like Trisha. Young, naive, an idealist with visions of what the future was supposed to be like.

"Phoebe made her decision and she's had plenty of opportunities to escape if she wanted to. She's chosen to stay with Noah. As crazy as that is."

He fell silent, his lips pressing tight and his expression looking as though he struggled with some inner pain. The pain of losing his sister to a cult?

Or maybe her words struck a nerve. What had she said exactly? What was it that led to this desperation?

Again, she ignored her growing empathy. "Go away. I'm tired and I don't have to answer any of your questions."

"Not even when it means saving someone else?"

She gave him a level stare. "If you think pushing guilt on me is going to crumble my resolve, think again. They want to be there. Besides, what are you hoping will happen? That she'll just leave and walk into some counseling service just because you've asked her to?"

He blinked, swallowed. "I don't know what to do. I'm at the end of my rope. If I weren't so desperate, I wouldn't have come here to ask you for help. I was hoping you could talk to her."

Her heart tightened, but she gritted her teeth. "I had hoped the same thing." She'd done more than hoped. She'd considered kidnapping, as dangerous and traumatic as it could be. Now Trisha was dead. "Leave your sister alone. She wants to be there."

With that, she walked away from the door and into the living room.

With rattled nerves, she sank down onto her secondhand couch. *Why, Lord? Why did You drop him into my life? He'll bring nothing but grief. Why do You want me to suffer so much? It's not fair.*

Lois Smith, her right-side neighbor, had told her to pray, but her gritty prayers had a petulant edge. And God never answered her, anyway.

The outside fell quiet. She liked the stillness, the peace it could bring. But today? No.

Abruptly, the phone rang and she let out a short cry.

Eli? Did he have a cell phone and was now calling her from her front door? Shaking, she listened to the insistent rings. Four, five… She snatched the receiver. "Leave me alone!"

"Kaylee, dear? What's wrong? Who was that man at your door?"

She sank against the wall. Lois. With their homes being so close, Lois's wisdom, along with her hugs and a hot cup of tea, were barely ten feet away. All that stood between them were some dying pansies and a chipped, cracked walkway.

No. Today, Eli Nash stood between them.

Kaylee fought back tears and after a swallow whispered, "That was Noah Nash's brother."

She heard Lois's little gasp. "Call the police, dear!"

"No. I think he left."

"I'll check." She could hear the older woman walk to her front window. "Yes, he's gone. Kaylee, dear, do you need some company?"

She wasn't the kind to grab company when it was offered, unlike so many of the friendly people here in New Brunswick. But Lois would provide a hug and a sympathetic ear, make the tea and offer advice if asked.

And if asked, the sweet old lady would suggest she help Eli. The Christian thing to do. Not what she wanted to hear right now.

Kaylee bit her lip, not wanting to snub her neighbor, and not sure she wanted to be alone.

"I'll be right over," Lois decided after the pause. "Let me put the dog out first. He hasn't been out yet today."

Minutes later, sympathy crinkling the skin between her sparse, graying eyebrows, Lois arrived. She held Kaylee's keys in her thin, arthritic hands. "I found this in the lock. Look at you! You've had a fright! You could use some hot tea." She bustled into the kitchen. Kaylee shuffled in behind and dropped into the nearest chair.

"What did that man want?" Lois asked.

She rubbed her forehead. "His sister's in the cult and he wants me to go back in to talk to her."

"Oh, my! What did you tell him?"

"I refused. I can't go back there." She watched Lois pour the tea, thinking of all those times she'd been monitored by the women in the compound. And ogled by some of the men. Never having a moment to herself.

It had pushed her, a natural introvert, to the point of desperation. Noah had known what would grate at her. She hadn't fallen under his spell as quickly as Trisha, but the months of poor food, cold nights and raw nerves had lowered her resistance. Then the unthinkable happened.

Noah had begun to make sense.

Lois squeezed her hand. "You'll get over this. Trust

the Lord. He'll do what's right. He knows where you are in your life journey and will meet you right there, if you ask Him."

"He's not moving fast enough," she muttered, disliking the words even as she said them.

"The pain of loss never goes away fast enough. You know, I lost a baby and my mother the same month, a long time ago. It took me years to get over the loss."

With a furtive glance over her mug, Kaylee sipped her tea. Lois always knew the right thing to say. Had her counselor subcontracted her work out to Lois? It sure seemed so.

The old woman smiled sadly. "But I had a wonderful husband, even if I had to share him with the army. He went to Korea, you know?"

"It must have been hard for him to leave." *Harder than me leaving Trisha that day, three weeks ago.* A knot of tears choked her as she remembered when Trisha had accidentally left her, and the back door, unattended. A split-second decision later, Kaylee slipped outside and then out through a gap in the chain-link fence. She went straight to the police.

Oblivious to Kaylee's memories, Lois chuckled. "I had a friend whose husband was going to Korea on the same ship as Walter. We were supposed to say our goodbyes at the train station, but my friend devised this plan to drive down to Halifax where their ship was waiting."

Looking conspiratorial, Lois leaned over. "Two women traveling all that way alone? There was no highway and her car was held together with rubber bands and a fast prayer."

Despite herself, Kaylee smiled. “What happened?”

“We broke down as soon as we reached Nova Scotia.”

“So you missed your husband?”

“No! An elderly man stopped to help. *He* drove us straight to the dockyard! Oh, he was as nervous as we were, not knowing who we were or what would happen.” She finished with a teary laugh. “We wouldn’t have made it to Halifax without that man!”

Kaylee’s lips thinned. “You’d have found a way.”

“No. The Lord sent us that man. God wanted him to help us, even if we did scare him. He was so sweet and a good Christian man to trust the Lord.”

Eli and his desperate situation filtered back to Kaylee. Phoebe could easily end up like Trisha. Her heart clenched. God may have been showing her that she was supposed to help Eli, but it was too late now.

Eli was long gone.

TWO

Kaylee struggled through work that next Monday. Eli's plea dogged her steps. Since she'd returned to normal society, she'd been fortunate enough to get a job in the town's recreation center. It paid minimum wage, but she hoped to find a better position soon.

She assisted the rec coordinator with everything from sorting well-worn sports equipment to brushing the autumn leaves off the basketball courts.

But working proved futile. On Mondays, she should be tidying up after the weekend's activities, but all she could manage was leaning heavily on her broom.

"You're in another world. What's wrong?"

She looked up at Jenn, her supervisor. "Bad weekend."

Jenn strode across the gym floor. "What happened?"

"I don't know. Stress, maybe?" Together they looked around the small gym. Kaylee hadn't done too much. "Sorry, I'll try to get the sweeping done before noon. I'm not lazy, you know."

"I know you're not. Don't worry about me thinking that."

Kaylee returned to her sweeping, holding back a sneeze when a stray draft threw some dust up at her face.

Jenn flicked her head toward the door through which she'd just come. "There's someone in the office looking for you. Why don't you take an early lunch? No hurry in here." With that, she turned.

Cold dread doused Kaylee as she watched the older woman leave. Someone was looking for her? Today?

No. Please not him.

She'd spent yesterday morning at church, having given in to Lois's gentle but persistent invitations. When she first came to Riverline, Lois had asked her to her Sunday services. She'd declined, even though the counselor she was seeing had thought it a good idea.

She'd had enough religion to last a lifetime.

But Lois had needed help bringing things to church and, feeling that she owed her kindly neighbor, she agreed.

Then Sunday afternoon she and Lois helped one of the seniors make some meals for the coming week. Throughout the day, Kaylee had even managed to keep away the guilt she'd felt whenever she thought of Eli. And she'd almost completely managed to keep thoughts of him far from her.

But now—

The door at the far end swung open. In walked Eli.

He had the same confident swagger as his brother. But where Noah preferred long hair, a thick beard and an air of mystery, Eli kept his hair short, almost a crew cut, and his smooth, square jaw gleamed, a handsome addition to a tanned and fit frame.

There was no mystery about what Eli wanted. He wanted Kaylee to help him. Period.

Their gazes locked. Natural light from the high windows proved complimentary to him. Despite the knocking of her heart, she tried her best to look unmoved.

She was not going to get caught up in a fascination of this man. Even if he was a law-abiding citizen wanting only to find his sister, Eli was still Noah Nash's brother. And Noah Nash had threatened her and forced her to do and say things that she still struggled with today.

Eli stopped a few feet from her, concern etched in his blue eyes. "I'm sorry."

She blinked. He was sorry? She hadn't considered that he might apologize.

A contrite smile formed on his lips. "I was way out of line on Saturday. My mother had told me not to contact you, but I did it anyway."

Kaylee felt a small surge of victory. She was right—vindicated by this man's own mother. "Even when she's so desperate to reach Phoebe?"

Eli straightened. "It does mean a lot to her to find Phoebe," he answered slowly, "but she didn't want me just barreling up to you. My mother realizes that you've been traumatized. She was worried I would ruin even the slimmest chances of finding Phoebe. But that's what I did anyway. I'm sorry."

She returned to her sweeping. "Apology accepted. If you'll excuse me, I have work to finish before lunch."

"Your boss said she'd give you an early lunch."

"She's feeling bad because of all I went through."

"You told her?"

She stopped her sweeping. "Like you said, I was on CNN. Must have been a slow week."

"Hardly. You were tortured for two years!"

"I wouldn't go that far—"

"I would. My brother kidnapped you."

"No. I went there willingly. I'd hoped to talk to Trisha, let her know I was worried. I figured she'd come home with me, if only for a short visit. We have mutual friends, an aunt who would have loved to see us…" She heard her words die off.

"But Trisha refused. Then Noah refused to let you leave. In that way, he kidnapped you."

Her grip on the broom tightened. "Noah decided that I could be useful."

"He threatened and manipulated you for two years. And that's the same as kidnapping, you know? He wanted someone who could help him with his cult. You fit the bill. You had to lie—"

She dropped the broom. The clatter of wood on wood rang harshly in the stale air around them. "How do you know so much? This is way more than CNN reported."

"I hired a private investigator who has connections within CNN. He was able to get a copy of the full interview."

She bit her lip. Yes, there had been an extensive interview and she'd been surprised and yet thankful that the majority of it had never aired. The interviewer had been good at her job, coaxing information from her. "Well, that's good for your investigator."

"He's the best. He also knew what to ask the State Troopers and the Houlton Police, too."

"He really earned his pay," she murmured.

"Yes, well, he also owes a few people, now. Look, I know that Noah saw an advantage in you staying there. I know he twisted the reasons around and threatened you to keep quiet and stay or he'd kill both you and Trisha. Then he got you to play the part of a prophetess."

She hated that part almost as much as losing Trisha. The shame of what she did and how she'd nearly fallen under Noah's spell still haunted her. "I'd rather not rehash it. Besides, this righteous indignation doesn't suit you."

He paused before answering. "It may not and I had no right to approach you with my requests. It was inconsiderate of me."

With a glare, she added, "So was coming here."

He stooped to retrieve her broom. If her harsh retort bothered him, he didn't show it. "You're right. But where my sister's concerned, I'm not always thinking straight." He handed her the broom and the moment stretched before them. A slight frown appeared when he blinked. "Phoebe means a lot to me."

Her own eyes welled up. Small and blonde, Phoebe projected an air of innocence and, to Kaylee's constant chagrin, total adoration of her brother, Noah.

"What's she doing for my brother, Kaylee? Tell me about her."

She shook her head. She'd built up an armor of resistance to the people in Noah's cult. No matter how much they loved being there or believed in Noah's vision of a new world or how much of a victim each might be, she'd layered on a disgust and dislike for all of them except Trisha. It had been a matter of survival for her when she realized how vulnerable she was becoming.

Begrudgingly, she answered, "Phoebe loves being there. Your brother has enthralled her. She believes in his vision of separating themselves from society because the world will soon end."

"Is that what you were made to predict?"

She folded her arms. "Among other things."

"Why? Why didn't you just tell them that you were being held against your will and you weren't a prophet?"

"He threatened to kill Trisha if I didn't do exactly as he said. At first, I didn't believe him. Then one day Noah had me brought down to the basement. There were only candles lit, so I couldn't see well." She steeled herself against the onslaught of harsh, ugly emotions. They still lodged hard in her throat, swelling until she felt breathless. "He told me in explicit detail what he'd do to Trisha if I left. From that day on, I had no doubt he would do it, too."

Eli shut his eyes. The frown deepened and his lips tightened to a tortured, thin line. "Phoebe has always looked up to Noah," he finally said. "She's not sharp or quick-witted. She's a baby, a victim. You know that, too. I can see it in your expression. Phoebe may be an adult, but sometimes adults are children."

In the counseling sessions she'd attended, she learned they were all victims of Noah's insanity.

And victims needed help.

But they'd all hurt her. By allowing Noah such horrible free rein, especially with her, they'd moved from victims to perpetrators. Her stomach clenched.

Eli opened his eyes and met her stare. Fighting the

unwelcomed guilt still rising in her, she returned to her sweeping, not before dashing away an errant tear. "Go away, Eli. Neither of us can help them."

She could feel him step closer to her. Too close. "We can help them. Phoebe needs you." His voice dropped to a whisper. "She's a victim just like you were."

Phoebe *was* too trusting. And too easily beguiled and willing to do anything for Noah, even if it meant hiding to prepare for the end of the world.

Kaylee struggled to fight the sympathy leaking in. And she struggled to fight the way Eli's words drew out the righteousness in her.

"Kaylee?"

She blinked back tears to focus on him. All she could see was gentle sympathy.

"I know how you feel. And I wish that what I was asking of you was easy."

He didn't know how she felt. "What are you asking, exactly? That I just talk Phoebe out of that cult? You sound like you think she'll listen to me. Considering what I've said and done and what Noah did to Trisha, I'd be the last person they'd open their door to, even if I did agree to go."

"But you know the compound. You know the house and grounds and everyone in there. You'd know how to get into it."

"So you need someone to tell you the layout of the house and then you'll just ask Phoebe to come outside?" She shook her head. "You'd have to be as smart as Noah to convince her to give it all up. Or as sly and shrewd."

Again, that hint of strife within him flitted across

his face. Only for the briefest of seconds, she noticed. Then it was gone. "I've been trying to talk to her for years. You're my best shot right now. I don't know what else to do. I've prayed about it constantly."

"Yes, well, prayer may be okay for finding a bit of temporary peace, but you have to be proactive or nothing works."

He frowned. "Why do you say that?"

"You better come up with a plan. Even if we get into the compound and then into the house, you still need to deal with those people. God only helps those who help themselves."

Eli frowned. "Is that what Noah taught you? God isn't some passive overseer. He's powerful, strong, willing to do anything to bring back His lost sheep."

"His lost sheep? He abandoned Trisha and let her be murdered!" she lashed out. "A drug overdose in a motel, the coroner reported. And everyone in that cult, Phoebe included, told the police Trisha was depressed because I left. They lied and said I was disillusioned because Noah had spurned me. I couldn't convince the police otherwise."

Her next breath caught in her throat and her head suddenly pounded. It was all so fresh, so hard to bear. "But it wasn't going to bring back Trisha and I wasn't strong enough to fight it all. I had to let it go, but believe me, it was the hardest thing I ever had to do."

When he didn't answer, when his lips tightened and she saw his throat bob, she glared at him. "Do you really think Phoebe's going to follow either of us out? You have to come up with something more drastic than that, I'm afraid."

He looked as if he wanted to say something, but

held it back. His face had become so easy to read. "You don't have a plan, do you?"

It was an accusation. She was angry.

He shook his head, barely. Allowing the surge of shock and anger to overtake her discretion, she burst out, "You're expecting God to step in with some divine intervention? That's admirable, but frankly, it's insane!"

"This is important to me, Kaylee. I can't explain it any more than that."

On her heel, she spun away from him to grab the dustpan. There was nothing left to say.

"Kaylee, I need to save my sister."

She pursed her lips to fight the compassion. She'd tried to save Trisha, even going to the police after she escaped, secretly hoping that their investigation would somehow free her sister. But they didn't take her claims seriously. "I tried to do the same." Her whisper rose as she continued speaking. "But the police believed everyone except me. Because I'd willingly stayed in that cult for two years, they didn't think I was held captive. And there was no evidence to back up my claim. All that I did to save my sister's life ended up condemning her to death!"

He didn't react to her outburst. "Do you go to the church in town? Is that where you were yesterday?"

Caught off guard by his question, she nodded. "I went because Lois, my neighbor, asked me to. She's been inviting me to go since I came. I didn't want to, believe me."

"Why?"

She gaped with shock at him. "Because, in case you

hadn't noticed, I've had more than my share of religion lately."

"No. You've had your share of a dangerous and evil man and his warped views." He wet his lips and with a look of concern, he tilted his head. She could see the faint scar he'd shown her on Saturday.

"Kaylee, you have to replace a negative behavior with positive behavior, right away. You have to be proactive when changing those thought patterns that lead only to the wrong attitudes and crippling fear."

"Like getting back on the horse when it throws you? No, thank you."

"No, not like that. It's important to replace negative thought patterns with positive thought patterns immediately, or else you risk being overwhelmed by your own fear and hatred. You can't ignore that part of you that hates everything that reminds you of Noah's cult. It's unhealthy."

When she said nothing, he asked, "What does your pastor say about suffering?"

"He's not my pastor. I just went to the church to please Lois." She bit her lip. "She said that we've all sinned. Yeah, except I didn't deserve what I got and I know Trisha didn't, either."

"If you disagree with the church, then why did you go?"

She shrugged. "Lois kept asking me to go and caught me at a weak moment. And she's been good to me since I came here to Riverline. But I think I should take a break from church for a while. Give myself time to heal."

"That's an odd thing to say," he answered with a soft smile. "Churches are famous for their healing."

She bristled at his little quip.

"Don't give up on church, Kaylee," he said softly. "That's like saying that Noah was right to form his cult, his own religion to suit himself. Don't let him win."

Kaylee bit her lip. She wanted nothing to do with Noah, ever again. She didn't want to think of him again, let alone face him. A shudder ran through her.

Eli leaned forward slightly. "What did your parents do when you stayed in that cult?"

"My parents are dead. My father worked on the oil rigs out in the Atlantic. One of them a few years back had an accident during a storm and he was swept overboard."

"I'm sorry. And your mother?"

"She developed lung cancer. She'd worked in a restaurant for years, supplementing the income and trying to stave off boredom, only to have all the second-hand smoke kill her."

"So no one missed you?"

"Only my aunt. But Trisha told me once that she wrote to her saying we were both fine and I'd seen the light and joined her group." The very idea that Trisha had lied and not felt guilty about it cut deeply into her. "She told me it was for my own good and that I'd thank her some day."

She pulled herself together. "Trisha was all I had left. But now she's gone, too." Her voice cracked and she hated the show of weakness.

Eli took her hand, as tenderly as his gaze held hers. "You can help Phoebe. She needs you. You can save another from Noah. I know it'll be the hardest thing you'll ever do, but you're my last hope. You couldn't save Trisha, but you can save my sister."

The armor she'd hardened crumbled as she stared in Eli's handsome face.

And found herself nodding.

Two days later, exhilaration still surged through Eli. He'd spent the last seven years praying for this and while Kaylee had declined his invitation to lunch to discuss what needed to be done, she had agreed to go with him to the compound early Wednesday morning.

So now, pulling into her driveway to pick her up, he smiled to himself again. *Thank You, Lord.*

His smile wavered as another thought hit him. What would Phoebe say to him when they finally saw each other? That he was being selfish and jealous again? That any time Noah had something, Eli wanted it?

Kaylee's appearance at her door dissolved the worry. She turned to check the lock, then trotted down the single step toward his car, carrying a small knapsacklike purse. Today, she wore the same jacket she'd worn on Saturday, but her pants were lighter, probably thanks to the warmer weather. Her dark hair was pulled back into a loose, wavy ponytail, something he felt would slip away if a strong wind or hand slipped into it.

A hand like his?

No. He shoved away the notion in time for her to reach his car.

As she opened the passenger door, she peered inside. "Are you expecting to be able to drive right up to the compound in this thing? It's too low to the ground."

"We'll go as far as possible, then walk in."

With a doubtful bite of her lip, she settled in beside him. Her knapsack remained in her tight grip. "We have to be careful. After what happened to Trisha, some of the locals are nervous about the compound."

"I imagine. They're as valuable to the border patrol as the surveillance cameras. There have been some pretty unsavory characters sneaking over the border." That was pretty much what his investigator reported. It was dangerous to live near the U.S.-Canadian border. Dangerous thanks to people like Noah.

Anger built in Eli and he fought it with a quick silent prayer. *Lord, take away my bitterness.*

"When Trisha died in that motel," Kaylee whispered, interrupting his prayer, "I knew it was Noah, but he'd managed to convince the police that Trisha missed me so much she deliberately overdosed and did so away from The Farm to save them from getting into trouble." She snapped her head over, her eyes hot. "He staged her murder to look like suicide! The police closed her file without another thought!"

Eli held his breath. What other dangerous things was Noah doing with his flock?

Keep Phoebe safe, Father. Use me to stop Noah.

The highway narrowed to two lanes as it wound through small towns at the western edge of New Brunswick. The border with Maine lay half an hour ahead, but Eli couldn't content himself with the passing scenery of quaint cottages, now closed for the season.

He cleared his throat. "How did Trisha get involved with Noah?"

"It wasn't him initially," she answered tersely. "It was another member. John Yale. Trisha was camping at Baxter State Park when she met John. He spent a lot of time talking to her."

John. So their second cousin still hung around. Eli

hadn't been able to confirm if he'd stayed on when Noah had moved his cult from Florida to rural Maine.

"He's an older man," she continued. "But for his age, he sure can climb mountains."

The strong, wiry John had been a fixture at family get-togethers and, taking a liking to Noah, would dream alongside him of running big companies and changing the world.

Eli gripped the steering wheel. Noah had always wanted power and control. Even as a child, he'd bullied and ruled their home. "So John recruited her there?"

Kaylee nodded. "Pretty much. Trisha was always an idealist. I told her once that she'd probably love to see the world blown up because then her ideals would be justified. We had a huge fight and didn't talk for weeks."

"We're you both living at home then?"

"Yes." She toyed with the straps of her knapsack. "In Nova Scotia."

"Did your parents always live there? How did you end up in the middle of New Brunswick?"

"My father worked on the oil platforms. He met my mother in Halifax and settled there. I took some college courses in agriculture and management and was close to securing a job up here at a local potato-processing plant."

He glanced over at her. "And you lost all chances when Noah kept you?"

"I'd been gone for two years and there wasn't much fight left in me. Plus, I'm still malnourished. That was Noah's way of gaining control over people. Hold back just enough food to ensure you're always hungry."

Eli's already firm grip on the steering wheel tightened until his knuckles ached.

Kaylee looked as if she could barely stand discussing this. Still, she said, "I came to the point where I just got used to the gnawing hunger. Everyone around me was the same way and they didn't complain."

He felt the uneasy pause.

"Certainly not in front of Phoebe or Noah."

He was at a loss at what to say. Finally, he murmured, "Doing without can make us better people."

"What good is doing without food?" She pulled up on her knapsack as she snapped, "It destroys the body and you're certainly not any better for it."

Guide my words, Lord, he prayed swiftly. "Have you asked your pastor about that?"

"I told you, Pastor Paul is not *my* pastor. I went to the church in Riverline because Lois asked me to and I owed her for helping me settle in. That's all."

He swallowed. "When bad things happen to Christians, we try to remember that our time here is miniscule compared to eternity in Heaven."

"Yeah, if you're good."

Eli shook his head. "No! You're saved by faith, not by works." He hadn't expected to witness to Kaylee and pulled a face as he tried to concentrate on his driving. And where they were going. "Do you like Lois's church?"

She took her time answering. "Yes. The people there are wonderful. They're kind and considerate."

"They're doing God's work—not for salvation, but because they love Him." He felt his tight grip on the wheel relax, hoping to give good answers without his full attention. "I wish I could take back all the awful things my brother did to you. You didn't suffer any permanent damage, did you?"

"Physically, no."

He knew what she meant. "Emotionally, you're strong, too. You're here today, aren't you?"

She twisted around in the seat and pinned him with a steady stare. "Were you kids raised in the church?"

"Mostly. I don't know the reasons for the breaks we took from church. Mom and Dad didn't discuss it. All I know is that Phoebe loved church and would become withdrawn when she couldn't go. Being the youngest and the church having some great kids' programs, she had all the fun. Our parents felt that Noah and I should sit through the regular service. We were treated as though we were the same age, even though he's eighteen months older than I am."

Noah bullied everyone. It wasn't until he started his cult that his parents saw that. By then, he'd taken Phoebe and hurt them all.

As if reading his mind, she asked, "How long have you been looking for Phoebe?"

"Actively? Five years," he answered.

"Searching must have been hard for you," she murmured. "But in all honesty, Eli, it's not going to be easy to talk to her."

The forest deepened and the quiet road narrowed. The sun retreated behind a bank of thick clouds and the brilliant fall leaves mutated into dark, ominous clumps.

"Then just get me in," he finally said.

"I won't be welcomed, you know. Noah was the only one who wanted me there. He called me Deborah, the prophetess. I was to reveal knowledge that he'd been secretly feeding me." Despite her derisive tone, her voice quivered. "I could barely handle it."

"But you did."

"It was either that or he'd kill Trisha." Her voice shook. "So I ended up doing as he said."

Eli glanced at her. He should pull over, take her and hug her. Tell her it's over; she's safe from Noah.

But was she? The border crossing had just appeared ahead of them. There was no turning around now. They were headed right back into the very danger from which she'd escaped.

He was as cruel as his brother was.

The border guard checked their identification and asked some basic questions that Eli answered just as briefly.

The whole time, Kaylee remained silent, probably thinking of the last time that she'd crossed the border, having escaped from the compound. Trisha had paid for Kaylee's freedom with her life.

And now he was taking Kaylee right back into that den of evil.

The guard handed back their identification and wished them a pleasant day.

Eli drove into the United States. Within minutes, they reached the main highway that ran parallel to the international border. A few moments later, he pulled into a small, rural service station.

"We need gas," he told her.

Kaylee peered warily around her. When she caught his eye, she explained, "I know what you're thinking. It's over. There's no way that Noah can hurt me again. Still…" She offered him a watery smile.

He found his heart pounding at her small smile. "I

won't let my brother hurt you again. We're doing the right thing here, reaching out to Phoebe. I know if I can just talk to her..."

Except he didn't know. He was just hoping... hoping for a miracle.

He glanced again at Kaylee's face. Tears flowed down her cheeks and he felt his heart clench suddenly.

"I—I'm sorry," she stuttered out, while swiping her face with the back of her hand. "I don't think I can do this, Eli. I'm not just scared of Noah. But also of myself."

Wariness prickled the hairs on his neck. "What do you mean?"

"There's something you should know."

THREE

Kaylee wished she could wipe away the alarm growing in Eli's expression. But he deserved to know the truth. Something she hadn't told a soul and had barely begun to acknowledge herself.

"What's wrong?" he asked.

She gnawed on her lower lip. "Going back there…I mean, it's not going to be easy. You have no idea…" She couldn't form the right words.

Eli reached across the console and took her hand. His palm felt warm and comforting on her cold skin and she wished she could cling to him.

No. He was a stranger, a brother of the man who'd killed her sister. As much as he, right this minute, offered warmth and comfort, she knew she'd have to be crazy to be swayed by his charisma. One forceful Nash was enough for any lifetime.

"Talk to me, Kaylee. Tell me what's going on." His voice turned smooth, soothing her raw nerves. She liked the way he said her name.

"Noah convinced everyone I was a prophetess," she whispered. "And, yes, he threatened me with terrible things to get me to say what he wanted. But it wasn't completely like that, not toward the end."

"I don't understand—"

She pulled back her hand, unable to focus on her thoughts while he held it. A tendril of her hair had worked loose. When it dropped against her cheek, she hastily tucked it over her ear and was glad for the distraction. "At first, some of the women asked Noah to kick me out because I was so adamant about being there against my will and they were tired of listening to me. But Noah refused. He was insane and power-hungry. To him, I must have represented the secular world and he wanted to be able to control it. I think he also must have thought that if he managed to tame me, it would send a message of dominance to the rest of his cult."

Eli's blue eyes snared hers. Deep within them she saw uneasiness. "How did he manage to convince you to stay?"

"His threats grew. At first I refused to listen to them, because they were vague and full of innuendos. Then they got specific that one day. And later, his threats against Trisha became too real. One day, she got hurt outside. A board fell on her from the top of the woodshed. Noah looked at me and I knew he'd staged it to show me he meant business. So I shut up. I was scared."

She paused, wondering why she was rehashing all the pain with this man, Noah Nash's brother, of all people. But then, a second later, the rest poured out of her as if a plug had been pulled from a sink full of bitter, dirty water. "The months of semistarvation, of cold, browbeating captivity. There came a point where

I just did what he said, period. I'd been taken to the lowest point in my life."

She struggled in vain against the tears and the humiliation that she'd just let loose with all her fears and pain. "Before I escaped, though, I'd actually started to believe what I was prophesizing." Shame added to the burn in her cheeks.

Through a swim of tears, she spied Eli climbing out of the car and walking around the front. He opened her door and tugged her to standing. Beyond, the gas attendant chose that moment to step out of the store.

Eli ignored him to pull her close. For a brief, delicious moment, she felt important, cared for. For that time, she didn't care who he was. He was what she wanted. Strong arms wrapped around her, protecting her. "I'm sorry," she mumbled.

"It's all right."

"Noah had started to make sense. The way he was interpreting things that had happened around us, the past and even what the Bible said. He'd started to really sound right."

Eli tightened his grip on her.

She cried for a while longer. "I don't want to go back there. I know what happened to me. I had started to believe some of the things he was saying. Then one day, Trisha left me alone in the kitchen. The back door was there and the yard was empty. I made this split-second decision to escape. I…I think it was just as possible that I would have stayed there. I don't want to go back. I don't want to risk getting trapped again."

He stiffened but held her tight. She felt his shoulders drop slightly. "I won't let anything happen to you. I won't let anyone hurt you or take you."

"What about Phoebe? What if Noah hurts her to get even?"

His mouth thinned and he tightened his jaw. "We just have to trust that she won't end up like your sister. That's all we can do."

"The day after I escaped, Trisha was found dead in that motel close to the border. It could happen—"

"Kaylee, I wish I could change the past, but I can't. You have to move forward."

Run. Leave. Go away. The urge to flee surged over her like a tidal wave. *Leave now while you still have a chance to prevent what could happen.*

She peeled free of his arms, giving him a push to put a few feet between them. "Easy for you to say!"

"Kaylee, wait!"

She stilled, but couldn't lift her gaze to his.

"Look at me," he said, the tone strong, full of command and confidence, yet strangely gentle.

She wound her gaze up his frame. Again, she saw only compassion in his eyes as he spoke. "I need you. Phoebe needs you. If she stays there, what'll happen to her? Or the other women in the group?"

She bit her lip and with her index fingers, wiped a few errant tears from under her eyes. While she was at The Farm, one of the women got married, with Noah officiating, of course, and she became pregnant. The baby was stillborn and they nearly lost the mother, too, because she had no prenatal care. Tiny Phoebe wouldn't survive if she got sick.

A knot formed in her throat as the attendant asked them if he could fill the tank. After Eli nodded, they moved away. "But what I did in there… What I said, and…and what I started to believe—"

"Don't think about that."

Her lips thinned as she formed a grim expression. Did he think she could just drop a thought like it was an unwanted bread crust or scrap of trash? He had no idea of the lies she'd been forced to say.

And yet, a voice within her asked, can you disappoint Eli? Or risk Phoebe?

Phoebe was Noah's most ardent follower, a voice inside reminded her. Think of the blow it would be to the group.

Kaylee swallowed. But Phoebe didn't have to be there, she argued internally.

Eli walked around the car, stopping only to thrust a few bills out at the attendant. "Let's go."

"I'm no good to you. Take me home."

After the young man left, he said, "We don't have time. We need to get to the compound. They go shopping on Wednesdays, remember?"

She blinked. "Yes, but how did you know that?"

"Remember, I have a very good investigator. He knows Noah nearly as well as I do."

She frowned. "Knowing your brother doesn't mean you know the cult's schedule."

Their gazes locked across the roof of the car. The hairs on her neck danced. Panic threatened again.

"Trust me, Kaylee. I've done my homework."

She narrowed her eyes. Finally, he went on, "Only the trustworthy women and one man to help were allowed to leave the compound. Noah used to tell everyone it was for safety and spiritual reasons. Should the end come, only being in the compound would save them, like being in the ark when the rains came."

He knew so much. "But you don't know if Phoebe

is going to be one of those that leave. Yes, Noah would trust her, but she could just as easily stay."

"That's where faith comes in. Let's go." He climbed into the car before she could reply.

They drove past a small picnic site, turned and then bumped over a culvert onto the next side road, heading east. She peered up at the low hanging branches that scraped the roof. The car dipped into a long rut, splashing mud over the bracken ferns that clawed their way onto the path. Like a drowning victim clinging to a lifeline, she gripped her knapsack.

"Hang in there," Eli said softly.

"The last time I was here, I was fleeing for my life."

He winced. Kaylee checked her grim satisfaction. She'd meant her words to be harsh. Noah was dangerous and Eli's faith wasn't going to help them. Nor would she trust her life to a God who'd allowed Trisha to die.

When Eli slowed down, his eyes alert, on the lookout for any visible activity, she searched for another subject to calm herself. "What do you do for a living?"

"When Phoebe went missing, I sold my business and devoted my time to finding her."

"Why did it take you so long?"

"Halfway through my search, I took some psychology courses and negotiation training. I actually got a short-term job working for a local police station."

The road straightened out and both of them fell back into silence. With the car crawling along the dirt road, Kaylee spent the time digesting his words.

Itinerant. Nothing to tie him down.

With her father gone so much when he was alive,

her mother found herself doing many things to stave off boredom, both Kaylee and Trisha had learned to appreciate security and stability.

Eli, a wanderer and one who could just hand over his life to the Lord. It was easy to understand how Lois could do that—she was a widow in the winter of her years—but how could he?

She stole a fast look at him. His handsome chiseled profile could lure a woman in. Under other circumstances, she might even have considered dating him.

No. She reined in that thought. He was a driven man who defined himself by his one noble goal—saving his sister. And once he'd achieved his aim, he'd be gone like a shot. He was one of those who were only in a person's life for a season—in this case, a short one.

The car bumped over some rocks, jarring her to the present situation. "We're getting close. I remember tripping over those rocks and some of the women would complain that they should be removed. Noah disagreed."

The tips of the rocks scraped the undercarriage, a terrible grating noise. "Of course. They serve as a natural early warning system." He slowed down even further, obviously trying to avoid any more detection. Branches scoured the doors, issuing more surreal screeches as they scratched the paint.

Kaylee nodded. Eli certainly knew his brother. She leaned forward, staring down at the road ahead. "Stop."

Eli stopped.

"No fresh wheel tracks, and it rained last night. No one's left the compound today." She paused, wracking her brain for a possible reason. "Up ahead, past those blackberry bushes, is a turnaround point. You'd better take advantage of it."

He maneuvered the car until it was safely facing the way they'd come. They climbed out as quietly as they could before Kaylee leaned over, her voice dropping. "After the next bend, you can see the compound. But they can also see you."

"Then we'll move off the path now." He headed into the thicket.

She held her breath, hating the anxiety growing in her again. "Setback city, here we come," she muttered.

Eli held back a branch for her. She heard him chuckle softly. "What may seem like a setback could be a test."

She stepped past the branch, tossing him a cool look as she slipped past. "And all your setbacks? There were bound to have been some. Did you call *them* tests?"

"Yes. The investigator couldn't find anything for years. It wasn't until CNN reported on you that we got a lead. I was so grateful for it." His voice cracked as he peered through the bushes ahead of them.

Unexpectedly, tears sprang into her eyes.

A bird called behind them.

Are You there, Lord?

Eli held up his hand. "I see it. Get down."

She knelt and, with a preparatory breath, looked up. Chain-link fencing, topped with barbed wire, encircled the overgrown old farmhouse and the two outbuildings that sat askew to it. One was a washhouse for the men, the other the men's quarters.

She'd never seen Noah enter or exit them. Driven and dangerous, he'd always stayed in the dark basement, keeping his face hidden. Trisha and Phoebe would say he was praying, but Kaylee couldn't help but wonder why he didn't do that in a warmer and drier room.

Driven and dangerous. Her heart hammered in her throat. Eli shared those same qualities with his brother.

Behind her, Eli's sharp inhalation drew cool air across her neck. Without warning, she was swamped with the urge to plow into him and stay safely huddled against his chest until this nightmare was finally over.

Caught between the compound that ruined her life and the man that could do the same again, she should run now while she had the chance.

"There's no one around."

Quickly, she scanned the area. "I don't even see the truck. Maybe it's been gone all night."

"What could they be doing?"

Shaking her head, she answered, "I don't know. Praying, maybe? Sometimes Noah would take them all to the basement for a prayer vigil. With him doing the praying, of course." Her last words turned derisive.

"Yes, it's called it *seeding.* With him controlling the prayers, he could be seeding his flock with specific instructions."

She shivered. "I remember the things he'd ask for."

Eli rubbed her arm lightly. "It's all right. You don't have to say any more."

"No." She shook her head. "You should know. Noah would take one of the flock and pray for them, claiming that it had been revealed to him that the person needed to have his or her wickedness purged."

"Sounds par for the course."

"Yeah, but it was me who delivered those lies." Oh,

how she hated what she'd done. Crouching down, she scowled at the drafty old farmhouse. The weather had been brutally cold last winter and everyone suffered. Even now, the memory chilled her bones. All those icy nights when she took pairs of socks or a sweater and jammed them in the leaks in the old bedroom window, anything to stop the drafts. Whose were they? Who complained in the morning when their clothes were stiff with frost?

She couldn't remember.

She didn't want to remember.

"I guess that's why God doesn't answer my prayers like Lois promised He would. I told awful lies for two years. I allowed Noah to intimidate me. My punishment, I suppose."

Her words had been soft, barely audible and not really meant for Eli's ears. But in the quiet woods, where even that lone bird no longer called, he heard. She should have kept her mouth shut tight.

"His grace is sufficient for you. You didn't need anything else, nor do you now."

With a twist around, she snapped at him. "Why are you quoting Scripture to me? It's as if—" She tried to curb her anger by shutting her mouth, but being here, knowing Trisha had died…the pain was still so fresh.

The knot in her throat tightened. She waved her hand. "Forget it. Don't answer. Let's work our way around back. Sometimes there's more life there." Without looking at him, she thrust through the dense forest.

Eli caught her arm. "Let me go first."

At the back, the forest encroached on the fence even more. If unchecked, it would soon swallow up the apron of cleared land skirting the chain link. Like the front gate, the back one was closed and locked with a huge padlock.

She looked up past it. The rear of the farmhouse lay as empty as the front. Kaylee's gaze wandered up to the second-floor bedroom, the one she'd shared with Trish and Phoebe for a short time.

She'd been a prisoner there, allowed out only for ablutions, the occasional meager meal and prayer service when her "abilities" as prophet were needed. Left alone for hours in that freezing bedroom with its cracked and drafty window. Trisha and Phoebe would join her at night. Most of those nights they'd all huddled in the same bed. Phoebe had often reminded them that the pioneers survived and they would, too. That God was preparing them for the hardships that come with starting a new world.

Evil propaganda fed to them by Noah.

"No one's around," Eli whispered. "Would the kids also be downstairs?"

Kaylee threw off the thoughts and shook her head. "No. The older ones would have taken the younger ones outside. There's no smoke from the chimney, either. And no chickens in the coop. This place looks like a tomb."

Eli drew in a sharp breath.

She cringed. "Sorry. Bad choice of words. Maybe we should get a bit closer."

Eli held up his hand and stood. Only then did she realize that he'd chosen his clothing well. His jacket, while not camouflaged, was a dark moss-green and his pants were chestnut. Only his pale blond hair stood out, but amidst the autumn golds and yellows of the birch and poplar, his coloring blended well.

He scanned the ground slowly, methodically, his gaze intent on finding something where trees met unruly grass.

Kaylee's heartbeat quickened through her temples. A wild mix of emotions barreled into her chest and out to her shaking hands. She leaned forward, casting wary glances around them. "They're gone, Eli. Taken off. Let's go. I don't want to stay here any longer than I have to."

He studied the yard, not answering her. Just as she leaned forward to tell him she'd wait for him in the car, he turned. "How did you get out of this yard? Did Noah leave the gate unlocked?"

She met his stare. His eyes were an incredible electric blue. Her naïveté reared and she wished she could read him. She sensed someone wanting desperately to find his sister, or at least desperate to get into this compound. But she also sensed something else and hated not being able to recognize it.

Finally, she flicked her head toward the south side of the yard. "Over there."

"Show me." He stood, stepped back and wrapped his strong fingers around her wrist. Then, twisting her around, he led her through the woods the way they came. She wanted to tug her hand free, but having someone close felt good, especially here.

They pushed through the thick woods and around the corner of the yard.

"Where?" he asked.

She stepped past him and scanned the fence. There had been a large bramble bush that had caught her clothing. The children had told her it hid the break.

There! She bent down and after pulling her sleeve

over her hand to protect it, she swept the prickly bush away to reveal the narrow break. When she turned back to Eli, his face was lit with anticipation.

"You may be too big to get through it," she commented.

"I'll manage." He bent back the chain link, tearing it up slightly from the ground. "You go first. I'll hold this back for you."

She hadn't needed him to do that, but once he stepped to the left, she swallowed down her reluctance and slipped into the compound.

She straightened. For a brief moment, Eli stood there, his eyes locked on hers. Wasn't he coming in, too? Doubt flooded her. Was he returning her to his horrible place—

No. His expression told of his own mixed emotions. Finding Phoebe, but in what condition? Or finding nothing but pain and a missed opportunity. Kaylee wanted so much to pull him into her and hold him tight.

She knew all about mixed emotions. That day she'd escaped, the jumble of dos and don'ts tangled into her reasoning. Then, in a millisecond, she'd made her decision and escaped. She knew the pain Eli was feeling right now, and wished she could somehow take it all away from him.

She drew in a breath, hating the sudden attraction that both lured and frightened her.

"We don't have to do this," she said softly.

"I need to." His expression melted. "And I'm glad you're here with me." Then he stepped through after her.

"Where first?" she asked.

"The house?"

She wet her lips. "I'd rather not, thank you."

"I told you I wouldn't let anything happen to you." He dusted off his pants, tugging free a dried bramble twig as he did so. "Okay, we'll do the outbuildings first. I wonder what they're for."

"The men sleep in one and wash up in the other. Only the married men were allowed to sleep in the house and only one man was married. Noah had strict rules about those sorts of thing. I don't know why, but I was glad."

"Perhaps abstinence was part of the starvation routine he used to wield his control."

Good point. She hadn't considered that, but it made sense.

Eli led her across the lawn to the front of the buildings. "Where does Noah sleep?"

"I don't know. He never slept when I was awake. He was always the first up and the last to bed."

"He always was a night owl."

She watched as Eli searched the men's building. It was much newer than the old farmhouse. Occasionally, she'd wondered what had been its original purpose. But she'd never heard the men complain about it. It must have been well insulated.

Finally, Eli came out. Without looking at her, he walked into the other one and within a minute, came out again.

The disappointment showed clearly on his face. The buildings were empty.

She felt her own heart sink and yet at the same time, relief sluiced through her.

Eli walked up to her. "There's no one in either building. The beds are made, everything is reasonably neat and tidy, like they just left it." He turned to the house.

"I don't want to go in," she blurted out. "Not into the house."

Eli blinked, his mouth softening from that tight line she'd seen before to something sympathetic. He reached out and took her hand. His fingers warmed hers.

"I know. But I have to find Phoebe. This is my life, Kaylee. And my parents need answers." After a moment of holding her hand, he dropped it. "I'll be back."

The wind slid across her face like strips of cold, wet cotton, the kind she'd used to wipe the dishes in The Farm when it had been her turn. Ahead, Eli stepped upon the rotting porch. She could hear it groan under his weight and the sound brought back a vivid memory. The day those who remained ate spring greens while the rest went grocery shopping. The woman who'd picked and steamed them had lifted her head sharply at the sound of those front boards relenting to Noah's weight.

Kaylee could still remember the look of apprehension on the two starving children who were still finishing their greens. When the door creaked open, the children gobbled up the rest on their plates and hurried to the sink. They dumped them in there and dashed out the back door.

"It's open," Eli said, breaking into her difficult memory. He pushed on the front door, then still outside, threw her his own version of that fearful expression.

Her heart squeezed. He didn't want to go in and find the cult dead, murdered by his brother or, just as bad, all having taken their own lives.

She pushed aside the terrible worry. This wasn't fair to Eli.

"Eli?"

Just inside the door, he turned.

"Maybe you shouldn't go in. Maybe we could call someone to search this place for you."

He frowned. "Like who? The police?"

She cringed. He knew her history, probably from the diligent investigator he'd hired. He knew she wouldn't want to deal with the police here ever again.

He shook his head. "Like I said, this is something I have to do."

Then, with gritted teeth, he walked inside.

FOUR

Tears diluted the scene before her. She didn't want to go inside her prison of two years.

But being out here, on what some might have been called the front lawn, wasn't desirable, either. Her mouth dried, then her throat. She swallowed hard in order to break the crackling feeling. Around her stood remnants of farm life; a rusting hoe and one of those rakes that tractors drag behind them. Propped against an old skeleton of a pickup was an equally ancient tractor wheel.

Her gaze wandered upstairs. From the room upstairs she'd looked down for hours on end, asking herself time and again if she'd break her neck should she try to escape through the window. She'd always stayed put, afraid that should she misbehave, she'd end up in that dungeon of a basement where Noah spent so much time.

A blue jay called out a shrill, indignant cry behind her and flew off to her left. To her right, the cause of the disturbance rustled the bushes.

It sounded big.

And it wasn't that far from the break in the fence.

From this distance, she could see the break and the crushed, waist-high grass and weeds where Eli had twisted the chain link. Whatever was following them would see it, too.

The rustling moved toward the break.

Her heart leaped and pounded in her throat and one of her mother's favorite sayings burst into her mind.

Better the enemy you know.

She broke into a run toward the house. Eli had left the door open and she leaped up past the squeaky plank, right to the stain where a welcome mat once lay and in the next step, over the threshold.

"There's no one in the kitchen."

She spun, so quickly she nearly lost her balance.

Eli didn't seem to notice her agitation. He'd already turned and headed into the living room. To her left stood the stairs. Up to her prison.

Get a grip, she scolded herself. *They're gone. No one's here. That rustling was just an animal.*

Eli appeared at the end of the hall ahead that lined the stairs, having walked the circle from the living room to the back hall. "Let's try upstairs," he said, his voice tight with anxiety.

"You fully expect to find someone here, don't you?"

He didn't answer. She barreled on anyway. "There's no one here, Eli. I can feel it."

"How so?"

"In the middle of the night when everyone was sleeping, or when they were gone for supplies and there were only a handful of us here, you could tell. There was life here. Now there's nothing." Her voice wobbled.

"You don't sound completely convinced. What's wrong?"

"I heard an animal outside, that's all. It spooked me."

With a frown, he studied her. "Noah wouldn't be noisy, if that's what you're thinking. You just said we're alone."

She bit her lip at his comment. She wanted to leave and to have Eli leave with her. But she knew what she'd said would only cement Eli's resolve to find out for himself. Not to prove her wrong, but to prove to himself that there was no one here, dead or alive.

He brushed off her comments. "We need to look for any clue to where they may have gone. Let's try upstairs, then work our way down."

She nodded, telling herself again that she was here for Eli. She'd agreed to get him into The Farm, to help him find Phoebe.

Eli swept past her and up the stairs. They all could be upstairs, but she doubted it. Even dead, she wagered that Noah and his cult would command a certain presence.

And there was nothing here. With a deep breath, she forced herself to remember that. And that Eli was here. She was safe. There was nothing in this house to hurt her.

The urge to run still burned in her. Swallowing it down, she climbed that first step with shaking legs. Then another step, each worn tread giving way to her. Without staring at Eli's legs as they walked upstairs, she knew he was there, guiding her in a way he didn't realize. "So who slept in what room?" he asked casually when he reached the top.

A moment of righteous anger surged through her.

Didn't he realize that this was one of the most difficult moments of her life, here and now? Couldn't he show some compassion?

At the top, Eli turned, fully expecting an answer. She stepped on the upstairs hall floor before giving him one. "Um, Phoebe and Trisha and I had this one." She pointed to her right. Each door of the five small bedrooms was closed. "The older women had the two end rooms and the kids slept there." She pointed to middle room.

He flicked his eyes from door to door. "There are five rooms up here." He looked at the one she hadn't mentioned. "Who had this one?"

"The married couple." She didn't want to think of them. They'd been the hopeful pair to lead the way for all of them to start a new generation. Except their plans hadn't turned out the way they wanted them to.

Eli shoved open the door of the room she'd shared. It was empty. Only then, did she realize she'd pulled in a breath and held it. Letting it out felt like a relief. She focused on her old room, noticing that all the furniture was still there.

It only added to the eerie atmosphere.

She found herself stepping into the bedroom. The bed was made, the threadbare bedclothes not quite as neatly made as she remembered. The cheap, thin pillows, three in a row on the double bed ahead of her, barely made a lump under the faded chenille bedspread. The whole room had a hasty-looking feel to it, not at all like Phoebe's usual meticulous standards.

She walked over to the window and looked down at the front yard. The same view as she'd seen so many times before.

Movement to her left caught her attention. That animal? Could it still be there, not scared off by her sudden flight into the house? She must not have made enough noise.

Like the silent house around her.

Silent? She cocked her head, listening. Hadn't Eli just opened a door? What was he doing?

"Eli?"

Nothing. She peeked one more time at the far view outside, but saw no movement or rustling in the woods that had closed in on the compound.

"Eli?" she called again.

Still nothing. Swallowing, she moved from the window, avoiding any accidental glance around the room as she slipped into the hall.

All the bedroom doors were open. "Where are you? Did you find anything?"

There was nothing but a chilling silence. She dared to peek into the next bedroom, then the far one and soon all of them. No one. Not even Eli.

She hadn't heard him walk down the stairs. They were old, and creaked—especially on cold, windy nights when falling temperatures and harsh eastern winds shifted the house.

Where was he? What was he doing? Trying to teach her not to be afraid of ghostly memories? To trust in God when there was nothing left to trust in?

Anger bubbled in her, followed swiftly by fear.

Maybe he'd left her in this house and that movement by the fence was him leaving.

His way to teach her a lesson on trust?

Just like Noah. The thought spat into her head and close on the heels of that accusation was another.

He was Noah. Eli Nash didn't exist. That was why Phoebe never mentioned him. He didn't exist. For all she knew, Eli was Noah's middle name and he was both left-handed and right-handed and had sought her out to avenge her desertion and fulfil his threats.

And Noah, now that he knew how she had escaped, was going to make sure she didn't escape again.

Tears burned her eyes. Her throat hurt from the choke of falling totally apart.

She had to get out of there.

Whirling, she flew down the stairs, missing the last two treads in a blind panicking stumble.

Two arms caught her. Firm, well-muscled, they wrapped around her torso and stopped her from falling on her face.

Pinned by them, she let out a cry and threw them off. "No! Let me go! What kind of sick lesson are you trying to teach me, anyway? You're insane!"

"It's me, Eli!"

Total panic flooded into her and her eyes widened in horror. "No, no! You're Noah! There's no such person as Eli! You're trying to trap me in here! To kill me like you threatened to do. I saw you!" She thrashed away from him, twisting until she was free.

"Kaylee! It's okay!"

She heard him, but couldn't control the fear racing through her. She flung herself at the front door, finding it closed. Then, firing it open, she fell over the threshold.

Eli shouted her name again. This time it registered, but she didn't dare listen. Gulping in the fresh fall air, she raced across the front yard, not headed to the cut in the fence, but straight at the gate.

She tripped over something and fell ungracefully on the dry, dormant grass.

"Kaylee, stop! You're going to hurt yourself. I'm not Noah! It's me, Eli!"

She saw him close in on her. Even now, with the panic settling in her, she couldn't stop herself. She knew the craziness of her actions, but she was beyond any self-control. She stumbled to her feet and began a zigzag trek around the house.

Reaching the back gate, she thrust out her arms and shoved hard. The posts, weakened by too many high winter snows, had lost their grip on the ground. One good shove from her and they toppled loudly, dragging brittle brush with them.

But they weren't so weak that they gave her full rein. She stumbled and crawled over them, only to have one post fight back. Her weight wasn't great enough to keep it down and she found herself scraped and tangled in the mix of chain link and barbed wire.

"Kaylee! What's going on? Are you crazy? Stop! You'll cut yourself to shreds!"

She stared up at Eli. He stood over her, worry frowning on his face.

There was no mockery, no smirk on his face. He held out his left hand and she saw the puckering scar he'd shown her before.

Confusion swept through her. Did Noah have that scar?

No, he didn't. She was sure now. "Where were you?"

"You mean, just now? I went into the basement."

"Why?"

"Looking for— Looking for any clues to where they went."

"Didn't you hear me call?"

"Once, but by the time I got up into the kitchen, you were already racing down the stairs. I had to grab you when you stumbled. You could have killed yourself."

Her panic drained away. "What did you find in the basement?"

He pulled in a deep breath and shook his head. "Not much. A table, a few chairs. It looked as if it was set up for one of those prayer sessions you described. A few candles. There was a lightbulb hanging from one of the beams."

A light? The times she'd been down there, only candles were used and she'd kept her head down in hopes no one would notice her. A shudder danced through her. Old knobby candles that smoked and stank and shot long shadows through the basement.

"To control us," she whispered. "He only used candles to keep us in the dark."

His lips tightened. "That doesn't surprise me."

She lay sprawled on the wire, looking up at him, trying to sort out her panic. "You didn't answer when I called and I didn't hear you go downstairs. I saw something outside..." She trailed off and her gaze flickered over to the break in the fence.

He followed her gaze. "What did you see?"

"The bushes move. Something deliberately stalking us, following us in."

He looked down at her. "Deliberately?"

She felt a warmth seep into her cheeks. "We'd made enough noise to scare off most wild animals. I—I thought it was you."

"Me?" A light of understanding dawned on his face. "You thought I was Noah, that I'd tricked you into revealing how you escaped." He shook his head, and she saw pain and hurt flit across his features. "I'm not Noah. And I don't ever want to be him."

"Neither Noah nor Phoebe ever mentioned you."

"I'd been chasing my brother, searching for Phoebe for years. Of course they wouldn't talk about me." He surveyed her grimly. "Now, we have to get you up, but don't move. You have barbed wire very close to your temple."

She rolled her eyes to her left. A sharp V-shaped piece of wire sat just inside her vision. Only then did she feel sting of the scrapes and scratches. She lay still as Eli gently freed her from the tangle of wire. He stepped on the fence, firmly enough for her to know he wanted her off it, too.

She reached out her hand. When he tugged her to standing, she glanced down. Her best pair of jeans was torn once at the left thigh and once along the outside of her right knee. The fence behind them lifted slightly under the release of the pressure from Eli's foot. They were outside the fence.

She watched him flick off twigs, her heartbeat slipping back to normal. Slowly, she recalled her crazy reasoning.

Crazy, it was. If Noah had lured her in with plans to trap her here, he wouldn't have been willing to go inside alone. He'd have lured her into the house.

And he would never have been so kind to her now.

Still bent over, Eli stared down at her feet. Curious, she followed his gaze to her well-worn street shoes.

"Kaylee."

She heard the warning in his voice and then saw what he saw. A thin wire had tangled itself around her shoe and leg.

"No!" He reached out to clamp his hand on her arm. "Stay still."

But she couldn't. "It's digging into my foot."

"Kaylee! No! Stay still!"

Too late. Jumping up, she flicked up her foot to toss off the wire.

Eli grabbed her and flung her down. Branches broke and gouged into her abdomen as she hit the ground. A second later, he fell on her.

A second after that, the ground around them exploded.

FIVE

The noise was deafening. Vibrations from the blast ripped through her body. She tried to rise, but Eli pinned her firmly to the ground.

"No," he whispered in her ear. "Not yet."

The acrid odor of burning chemicals stung her nose. She blinked, but it hurt even to keep her eyes closed. Heat roared up her, a whooshing, searing wave blocked only by Eli's big frame. He shoved her arms under her body to protect them. His short hair bristled against her ear as burning debris rained down on them.

Then, abruptly, everything stopped. Eli lifted his head and she could feel him above her, scanning the woods. "Ready?" he asked.

She opened her eyes. "For what?"

"To run." He paused, then leapt to his feet, dragging her up with him. "Run! Straight that way! And don't stop!"

He pointed and pushed at the same time and Kaylee obeyed immediately, despite the question of why ringing in her head. It was answered immediately. Another series of explosions rocked the woods around them. They both jumped, but continued to run, snapping branches, galloping over fallen logs and moss-covered rocks. Fear pumped energy into her legs and she used it to push deeper into the woods, away from the compound.

Another blast tore up something big behind them and, yet, it sounded farther away. Because she was running? Or had this blast been at the other side of the house? The car, maybe?

She didn't stop to see. She kept slashing her way wildly through the thick, untouched forest, widening the distance between her and Eli. Her heart pounded in her throat, beats so rapid they drummed a steady blur against her tight windpipe.

Finally, she stumbled to a halt, panting as her burst of energy suddenly waned. Turning with her hands on her knees and lungs on fire, she scanned the way she'd come for Eli.

Where was he?

Had one of the blasts got him?

The branches she'd slashed through parted. Eli, well camouflaged in his clothes, stepped into sight.

She sighed. When he reached her, she managed to croak out, "What was all that? Bombs?"

Panting himself, he nodded.

"Where did you go? You were right behind me."

He offered her a short smile. "I didn't expect you to be Olympic sprinting material. I stopped once to see if the explosions were moving in a circular pattern, which they were, ending at the house. When I turned back, you'd already passed the border."

She glanced around. "We're in Canada?"

"Yes. Don't you remember passing a clear-cut line? There was a stone marker, too."

She blinked. Her beating heart and panting breath choked off her answer. All she could manage was a shake of her head.

"Let's go."

She looked up at Eli. "Where?"

"Back to the car, if it's still in one piece. I have a cell phone there. We should call the police and the border patrol, if they don't already know what's happened. We'll have to give the area a wide berth. There could be more unexploded devices still there."

"Still some left? The whole compound must have exploded! There won't be anything left!"

"We still need to call the police."

Refusing to move, she threw up her arms. "Why? Give me one good reason why *I* should talk to the police. They did nothing to help me when Trisha died. I told them she was murdered, but they said there was no evidence. They weren't interested in helping me and I was too beaten down to try to convince them. I'm not going to bother talking with them now."

She stalked away from him, smacking back branches still clothed with the yellow leaves of autumn, all the while feeling Eli's eyes on her back.

"They'll believe you now."

She stopped. Eli held his breath. *Turn around, Kaylee. Stop fighting the life God has given you.*

In the distance, cutting through the autumn stillness, a siren wailed.

Still, Kaylee refused to turn. Strangely, her actions hurt him.

But why? Because she refused to do what he knew was right? Because she wasn't a Christian?

Slowly, she turned around and Eli found himself exhaling in relief. She took several hesitant steps toward him before she spoke.

"I hope they believe me. And the only reason I'll talk to them now would be because it's justice for Trisha. And to show them I'm not that petulant woman who Noah supposedly spurned." She straightened her shoulders and nodded.

Yes, she wanted justice for her sister and rightly so. But she also wanted to prove to the police that they were wrong about her.

He was only here to find Phoebe. At any cost, too. Something sharp dug into his heart. He inhaled. Was Phoebe right when she accused him of selfishness?

He swallowed, looking down at Kaylee's dark hair and pale, exotic features. How she could be of English origin, he wondered suddenly. Her eyes were dark, mysterious and she looked very much the Biblical prophetess. Noah must have seen the advantage she could give him.

Eli shut his eyes. Was he doing the same thing here?

"All right. We'll go back. But," she told him quietly but firmly, "you may have to face the fact that Noah could have killed them all. If not here, then somewhere else."

With gritted teeth, he said, "Don't you think you're just avoiding the issue here? I know you don't want to confront Noah again, but that could be our only solution. You can't run away from it."

"I'm not running away! But a person doesn't stick their hand out again after the dog has bitten it!"

"Not even if it could save someone else? Would you

think this way if Trisha were still alive? If you think that these people are beyond help, why did you try to talk her into coming home in the first place?"

He hated his argumentative words as soon as they left his mouth. Arguing wasn't going to help them. Or help Phoebe.

Phoebe. Could she really be dead? Would Noah kill her because he knew his brother would soon find them?

The sirens grew louder, their baleful whine cutting through the woods. Finally, one stopped. They had either reached the car or the compound.

Eli kept one ear listening for the other sirens to stop, too. And the other listening to Kaylee's silence. She still hadn't answered him. Only the thin line that was now her mouth showed him that she was as determined as he was.

Finally, she said, "I didn't know they were beyond help when I first went there. But I know that now. I'm sorry if that's not what you want to hear."

He stepped closer, shaking his head, trying to sound reasonable, logical, while fighting the images Kaylee had suggested. "You could be right, but don't leave. You're miles from the nearest phone and I don't think you're the kind of person who would stroll up to a stranger's house and ask for help. Once the authorities realize that you haven't gone back through customs, they'll find you and rehash everything again. Do you want that? You know they'll wonder if it was you here today."

The forest around them was slowly coming to life again with birds determined to spend the coming winter there. The breeze had dissipated the stench of the explosions and one by one the sirens died. For a moment, Eli felt tempted to forget all that had happened.

With a pained frown, Kaylee shut her eyes.

Hating that his words, as true as they were, could hurt so much, Eli turned her back toward the compound. It would be easy to follow their tracks through the woods, with bent branches and disturbed forest fall showing their wild flight. And it would be easy to just stand there a moment and hold her close. Until the police found them.

He said nothing as he led the way back, but his mind whirred. Noah had warned that he'd kill Trisha *and* Kaylee if she left. Were these explosions part of that threat?

"Stop."

Eli looked up from where he'd been picking his way through the woods. A border-patrol officer stood about ten feet away, leveling his pistol at them. Sighing behind him, Kaylee stepped out to Eli's right.

"Don't come any closer," the officer warned. "This area is booby-trapped."

"We know," she said, her voice tired.

The man frowned. "May I ask what you two are doing here? You realize you've crossed the border illegally."

Eli nodded. "We're the ones who tripped those explosives. I told Kaylee to run so we wouldn't get blown to pieces."

After holstering his weapon, the officer keyed the mike on his radio and spoke into it, quietly. A garbled voice answered him. Finally, he said to them, "What were you doing here?"

Kaylee spoke. "I'm Kaylee Campbell. My sister

was part of the cult that lived here until she died three weeks ago. Trisha Campbell? You must have heard of her. She was found in a motel in Houlton, dead." She threw a nervous glance at Eli. "We came back to find his sister."

The officer looked at him. "And who are you?"

"Eli Nash." He gave the man a grim look. "There's a lot to tell you, so we'd better find the police. I don't really want to repeat it any more often than necessary."

Two hours later, Eli looked tiredly across the table at three men.

"Mr. Nash, why do you think your brother booby-trapped his own compound?" The state police officer asked the question, while both he and the border-patrol officer stared coolly at him. Another man, an explosives expert, Eli suspected, stood at the door. Kaylee sat perched on the seat beside Eli, and he felt a protective urge growing. To protect her from these men? Or the horrors they could reveal and rehash?

They were all packed in a small room in the Houlton Police Station. While the authorities might act cool, Eli knew they were nervous. They had a death that may need another investigation. And a series of explosions to deal with. Lots of dangerous, unanswered questions, and probably the media hovering outside the building, pressing for their own answers.

He leaned forward. "Let me ask a question, first. How long ago do you believe those bombs were set?"

"How long do *you* think they'd been there?" the state police officer countered.

"I noticed some broken branches and crushed grass around them, all fresh. I'd say a day or two."

The police officer nodded. "It looks like they were set within the last few days. Now, answer my question. Why would your brother blow up his own compound?"

"He knew I was looking for Phoebe. He must have known I was getting close, probably because Kaylee's story made it to CNN."

"But he could have just abandoned it without mining it," the explosives expert said. "Why scuttle it?" This man was a soldier trained in explosives disposal, meaning the police felt this was enough of a threat to call in the military.

Eli glanced at Kaylee. She looked as if she needed to search for the right words. "We can't explain Noah's reasoning," she began. "All I can tell you is that he's crazy, plain and simple." She glared at the man.

"We just want the facts," the man answered quietly, "and any information you can provide, Miss. That includes what kind of person we're dealing with."

She bristled and, in Eli's opinion, rightly so. "You've already met Noah, but at that time, he'd played a rational, pious man for you. And duped all of you. While I looked like a woman on the verge of a meltdown." Immediately, she stopped. Eli held his breath as she threw a cautious look at him.

He focused on the police officer. "Noah threatened Kaylee's life and he knew that her exposure on CNN would bring me here. He likes to toy with people, as a cat plays with a mouse before killing it. I'm his brother. I know what he's like."

"How long has it been since you last saw him?"

"Seven years."

"And you don't think he's changed in that time?"

"No." He folded his arms.

The police officer rubbed his jaw, obviously mentally sorting out the details. "Then why would your sister choose to stay with him?"

Eli's head was starting to pound. "He's persuasive."

"And he killed my sister!" Kaylee interjected.

"There was no proof of foul play, Miss Campbell. I'm sorry."

"Because Noah Nash is a cunning, intelligent man." She glared at the officer. "And he probably hoped Eli would be blown up with the explosions. When he says he'll do something, he thinks it through very carefully. He warned me he'd kill Trisha and he did!"

"Were you in love with him?"

"No!" Exasperated, she threw up her hands. "How can I convince you people that I hated him? He kept me locked up for two years! Those followers of his all lied about me because he told them to. And you believe them instead of me!"

"So why are you now trying to free one of those followers if they're so dangerous to you? If they held you captive, wouldn't you *not* want to go back and risk being kidnapped again?"

Kaylee fell silent. Eli watched her swallow, knowing the police officer had backed her into a corner. A tear slipped down her cheek.

Before he could speak in her defense, she said, "Besides the fact that they're victims themselves, I decided to help Eli because I didn't want him to go through what I did when I lost Trisha. But believe me. It wasn't an easy decision."

The officer's expression softened slightly. "But if

you knew Noah was so dangerous, why risk confronting him again?"

Kaylee cast her gaze downward. Cold dread washed over Eli. Yes, Noah hadn't just threatened to kill Trisha, should Kaylee escape. He'd threatened her, too. She'd risked so much returning there. Her life and, as she'd admitted to him, her beliefs and, yes, her personal freedom.

All because Eli had convinced her. And maybe she was, like him, relying also on God for help.

Eli wanted to drag Kaylee out of there, right that minute. Take her someplace safe. He snapped his head toward the officer. "Do you know where Noah is now? He's taken them back to northern Florida, hasn't he?"

The officer grilled him with a hard stare that matched Eli's tone. "Why do you say that?"

"Educated guess." He leaned forward. "All I want is to talk to my sister. Cut me some slack here, please."

The men looked at each other.

Encouraged by the hesitation, Eli plowed on. "Don't protect Noah. Not after he set those explosives."

The older officer spoke. "They stopped for gas near the house. One of the children mentioned to the attendant where they were headed, who said they could go a bit farther and see some great theme parks, but the kid had never heard of any of them. That's how come the attendant remembered them."

Eli blinked, his breath locking itself in his lungs as he digested the police officer's words. The boy who'd filled his tank knew where they'd gone?

Wait. He knew his brother. Noah wasn't heading south for the winter. Maybe the rest, but not him.

Beside him, Kaylee let out a long breath. A premature breath, but now wasn't the time to tell her so.

"I still don't understand why Noah would blow up his own home," one of the officers said. "He could toy with you doing something less risky to himself."

Eli stood, slowly, his mind whirring. With what the police had just said, it wouldn't be hard to find Phoebe.

No longer a cold trail. He'd missed Phoebe this time, but—

All eyes in the room fell on him. Cold dread began to trickle down his back. "He threatened to kill Kaylee. And he wants me to stop searching for our sister because I'm the closest thing to a threat to him. Booby-trapping his own home could kill two birds with one stone."

And, Eli thought grimly, Noah wouldn't give up.

SIX

No one spoke. Eli waited, hearing only Kaylee beside him, as she let out another thankful sigh. Relief because she believed Noah was gone.

Eli knew he wasn't, but he had no proof. And what about Phoebe? It wouldn't be hard to find her. The trail was no longer cold. A few phone calls and his investigator could easily learn where she was headed.

Except, what about Kaylee?

"Why do you say that?" the policeman asked. "Do you have any proof he wants you both dead?"

"Nothing, except his threats."

With a hint of skepticism, the officer turned to Kaylee. "What do you think?"

She moistened her lips. "It's over. And I'd just like to go home."

Across the table from them, the officer gathered up his pen and paper. "I'll need an address from each of you, should we need to ask more questions."

"Of course."

The addresses given, they were allowed to leave. Outside, the evening had turned crisp, with sharp chips of bright stars overhead and the feeling of frost slicing through him. When they reached his car, he offered another short prayer of thanks that it hadn't been destroyed, then turned. "We need to talk."

Kaylee stopped. Several people walked past them. A few dry leaves, shed from the trees by a rogue wind, crunched underfoot.

She turned. "What's there to talk about?"

He took her arm, discarding any gentle sympathy he might have. This was too serious an issue to sugarcoat. "We have to talk about what happened back there in the farmhouse. By the door. Among other things."

She fidgeted. "I thought you were Noah, but I was wrong. Noah would have abandoned me there, then detonated the explosives. You came up from the basement. I remember hearing you now." She yanked her arm free and reached for the passenger door.

"There's more, Kaylee. And you know it."

Her hand stilled on the handle. He leaned forward. "You thought I *was* Noah."

"I was mistaken. I just said that."

"You accused me of trying to teach you some kind of sick lesson. Do you need to talk about this?"

"No."

He needed her to trust him. Her life was on the line and he would not allow Noah to destroy it.

"I'd rather we not discuss it," she added. "I'm tired and I want to go home. I know it's late, but would you please drive me home?"

"I could find us a couple of rooms in a motel here—"

She spun around. "I've had quite enough of the motels here! I'd rather go home."

Trisha. How could he have forgotten? He could

have kicked himself for his stupidity. "I'm sorry. Yes, I'll take you home. But first, what sick lesson were you talking about?"

She rubbed her temples with her fingers. He waited, the wind chilling him. The leaves from a nearby maple flew around, several snagging the windshield wipers of his car.

Finally, she whispered, "The sick lesson was on trust. A lot of Noah's sermons talked about that. Trust in him, of course, as the voice of God. But…you know…God?"

"No." He shook his head. "I don't understand."

Exasperated, she smacked the car window. "I thought you were trying to *make* me trust God!" She made a disgusted noise. "I don't know! I thought you were trying to scare me because I didn't trust God enough. Except I thought you were Noah. And Noah would say trust in him was trust in God."

She folded her arms, rubbing them lightly with her hands. "I thought you were horrible to do that."

He touched her chin and tilted it to face him. To his surprise, his heart was pounding hard. "I would love for you to trust God completely. But that's not easy, even for a lot of Christians."

Her eyes widened, catching the yellow glow from the streetlight. She blinked, once, twice, then swallowed.

He yanked back his hand, choosing instead to run it through his hair than to touch her. The short ends scraped against his palm. Frustration tightened the muscles in his neck. "But I would never use a sick lesson to teach that. I would…"

He heard himself trailing off. He'd brought her

here, done everything short of kidnapping in order to get her to show him the hidden way into the compound. She could have just told him where the break was, but he'd expected that she'd want to be part of Phoebe's liberation. And he practically dragged her here, hoping she could somehow help.

And she'd tried, against her own fear and better judgment. It didn't make him feel any better.

"It may not have been a sick lesson, but what I did was just as bad," he said, half to himself. Then he focused on her face, as she pulled her jacket closer to her neck. "And I would never pull a stunt like trying to be someone else."

She held her jacket collar close and refused to meet his eyes. "I know that it wasn't you. Now, anyway. But before...I thought you were Noah and...I thought I saw you out in the yard, moving around." She shook her head. "But it was probably an animal."

He quirked an eyebrow. "You mistook an animal for me?"

She smiled briefly, acknowledging with some embarrassment the attempt at humor. "No. I panicked. Never mind."

A cold breeze found a break between his collar and his neck, driving a chill down his spine. Could Noah be that close? No way. He'd have triggered the explosives while they were still in the house, not waited until they'd escaped over the fence.

"It was probably just an animal. Raccoons can make quite a racket for their size." He unlocked the passenger door. "Let's go."

The drive home was long, excruciating and deathly silent. Out of all she'd said, even that she'd thought he was Noah, one thing lingered in Eli's mind throughout the drive. That she thought that trusting in God was horrible. Or even teaching someone such. Sure, the method she'd mistakenly thought was being used was just plain wrong, but still, the dislike of even trusting in God had been harshly evident in her tone.

Any advice, Lord? I sure could use it now. His casual prayer sounded impudent and he cut it off sharply.

Lord in Heaven, guard my thoughts. Give me the words I need to minister to Kaylee.

All he felt in the quiet of the car was a sense of patience trying to reach into him. *Wait,* the Lord seemed to say. *Patience.*

Patience with Kaylee? Or for finding Phoebe?

But for seven years, he'd been patient. More now? With Phoebe gone who knew where? He didn't feel like being patient anymore.

It was well after dark when Eli finally turned off the highway to head into Riverline. They passed the motel where he'd taken a room. But the edge to the evening told him that he wouldn't sleep there tonight.

He'd be watching Kaylee's house instead.

"I'm sorry you didn't find Phoebe," Kaylee told him softly as he pulled into her driveway. "What are you going to do now?"

"If you don't mind, I think I'll stick around for a few days. I have some calls to make and it'll be easier if I stay in one place."

"Suit yourself." She climbed out, grabbing her small knapsack and eyeing him with caution as he thrust his own door open. "I just know that I'm planning on sleeping a whole lot better knowing that Noah is far away."

He walked her to her front door, contemplating whether or not he should remind her of what he'd said back there in the police station about Noah wanting her dead, as well. Should he ruin one decent night's sleep for her?

Instead, he asked, "How do you feel now that the whole compound is gone? The buildings, house, everything?"

"Relieved. Plain and simple." She studied his face. "Why? How do you feel? I'm sorry I said that stuff about Noah killing the rest of them." She tried a smile. "But we, I mean, the police dog, didn't find any bodies."

"Thank you." The night breeze had picked up a chill from the river and he knew he should let her go inside.

But being here with her…felt normal. And for a long time, nothing in his life had felt that way. Suddenly, a part of him didn't want to remember that Noah may not have fled south.

He cut off the thought. No. He had to stay very aware of that fact.

"I'm glad that there was no one in the house," he answered quietly.

"But you're not happy that Phoebe's gone."

"True. She's still alive, though. I'll find her." He stepped back onto the narrow sidewalk leading to her little house. "Will you be at church on Sunday?"

"You weren't planning on staying that long, were you?"

He lifted an eyebrow and watched her cheeks redden in the glow from the streetlight above his car. "It may take me a few days to get the information I need, and I'd like to see your church."

She hastily unlocked her front door. "It's not my church. But of course, they'd welcome you. I tease Lois that she's always looking for fresh blood."

He smiled and she returned it immediately. He could feel how relaxed she was and wished he felt the same.

He should remind her of his concerns. "Kaylee, there's something you should know."

Immediately, a dog nearby started to bark. The insistent yelping sounded like it came from the back of her house.

"That's Lois's dog, Pepe. He's always sneaking into my yard. I think the previous tenant used to feed him."

The dog's barking turned frenzied. With a shake of her head, she pushed open her door. "I better call Lois. She's the only one who can settle him down, but I think she's a bit hard of hearing, so she doesn't always know what he's doing."

Twisting around, she caught the light from the street. She looked much like a teenager, a scared, wide-eyed one who'd seen too much for her young age, one of those haunting girls who might grace the cover of a missionary magazine. So cautious, so wanting to trust, he felt the image burn into his brain. He cleared his throat, unsure of what to do with the emotions churning inside of him. "I'll say good-night now and see you Sunday, then."

She hesitated. "I don't know. I've been so tired lately and a chance to sleep in..."

"No," he said, stepping a few inches closer, "don't shut out this opportunity. Don't let Noah win here. You should see and prove to yourself that this church can help you. And that Noah was wrong. About everything."

"You don't know anything about that church. How can you say that?"

Gut feeling? God-given? Instead of those answers, he gave her one of logic. "Lois cares for you and she goes to that church. I've heard what some people in town say about the congregation. Don't judge them prematurely. It's not fair to Lois or the people who can help you."

She dropped her head slightly and sighed. "I don't want to prejudge them."

"Good. I'll see you there." Then, smiling, he added, "Good night."

She didn't return it. Eli watched her close and lock her door. He walked back to his car, all the while listening to the dog's frenetic barks growing wilder. A few minutes later, a door opened at the next house and he could hear Lois call her pet.

As he climbed to his car, the dog stopped barking. He tapped the steering wheel, torn between going back to Kaylee's house to tell her his suspicions and letting her have one good night's sleep.

Leave her alone. She needed some time to digest all that had happened. It had been a brutal day for both of them. He hadn't expected the explosives anymore than she had. Only working with the police taught him to be wary and to recognize danger.

Dropping his head down on the steering wheel, he shut his eyes. The prayer he tried to form came out jumbled, chaotic, but he knew that wasn't important. He just didn't seem to have the strength to sort out the right words.

Grimly, he backed out of the driveway, drove down the street and parked in front of a small convenience store that had closed for the evening. From there, he could see Kaylee's house and the street that intersected her cul-de-sac.

He waited, too drained to do anything but shut his eyes.

A sharp rapping jolted him. Turning, he winced at the blinding light in his face. When the flashlight dropped, he blinked into focus the time on his car stereo. Seven something.

He'd fallen asleep. He'd been watching her house and drifted off. Automatically, his attention shot to Kaylee's house, beyond the police car that was parked broadside to him. It looked no different than last night, except that her lights were off.

"Want to get out of the car, sir?"

He peered at the nametag of the police officer staring in at him. Auxiliary Police Officer Jim Reading, it said. From the looks of the burly man, he was older, maybe retired from the military or regular police force. Eli climbed out.

"Did you spend the night in your car, sir?"

"Yes, I did."

The officer asked for registration and driver's license, which Eli provided. That done, the man asked, "Why did you spend the night here?"

"I wanted to keep an eye on Kaylee Campbell's house."

"For what reason?"

"My brother threatened her and I believe he'll carry out his threat."

"So you don't believe he's gone south?"

Eli's brows knitted together quickly. "You know him?"

The officer didn't answer right away. *Of course.* Kaylee had told the state police where she lived. They would call to confirm her address and offer a courtesy call to let the police here know what had happened.

"We had some water bombers on standby to douse any forest fires that may have started from the explosions. The bombers scoop up water from the river, so they usually let our detachment know their plans." He tilted his head to the left to study Eli. "But I don't think it's wise to follow Kaylee around."

"Have I broken the law being parked here?"

"No. You just made a few of the residents of this street nervous, that's all. They woke up to see the same car there as the night before." He tucked his flashlight away and folded his arms. Eli noted that they were equal in height. The officer met his gaze with something more than just politeness. His tone changed, softened slightly. "It's okay to be concerned for a friend, but wouldn't it be wise to let us know?"

Good advice. But he'd spent the night supposedly waiting for Noah to show up. He could have easily put a thousand miles on his car, heading south, following a trail that would hopefully lead to Phoebe.

Instead, he'd stayed here and had promptly fallen asleep.

Rolling his shoulders, he said, "Thank you. I think I'll just go check on Kaylee."

The officer stopped him with a firm hand. "*I'll* go check on her. You can get yourself some breakfast and find a motel room, if you plan to stick around."

He had a motel room, but had hardly used it.

"Thanks." He turned toward his car, then turned back. "How well do you know Kaylee Campbell?"

"Well enough for a small town. But, take another piece of advice, Mr. Nash. Your brother's gone, so you should be, too. Kaylee has enough to deal with. You're only making things worse."

Yes, he probably was. But he couldn't just walk away now. Not with all that had happened. Not with the memory of Kaylee's wide, exotic eyes haunting him.

"Time to move on, Mr. Nash. Either that or find a motel and clean up. I'll go check on Kaylee."

As the man turned to go, Eli said, "Thank you."

The officer turned back to him, pulled out a card and scribbled something on it. He handed it to Eli. "This is my cell number. You can call it anytime if you're worried about Kaylee. We all care about her. She hasn't been here long, but she's become like family to my aunt. She's her neighbor, Lois Smith. So I know how much Kaylee wants to start again."

Reading dipped his head once, then climbed back into his cruiser.

Eli watched the police officer drive up to Kaylee's little bungalow. A moment later, he was knocking on the door. A moment after that, Kaylee answered it.

He found himself sighing. When the officer pointed down the short street at him, he climbed back into his car. Even at this distance, he could read her body language. Her stiff shoulders, her tightly crossed arms. She didn't like his concern.

So what else was he supposed to do? The police officer nodded, returned to his car and drove away. He watched the cruiser roll past him.

Movement caught his attention. Kaylee shook her head before returning inside.

He drove up to her house.

She opened her door before he reached it. "You spent the night in your car? Are you nuts? You could have frozen to death!"

"We're having an Indian summer. It wasn't that cold. Plus, I have a blanket in the back."

Disbelief lingered on her face as she shook her head. "Why? Why did you do that?"

"Because…" he started, then cut off his words. Kaylee wouldn't believe him if he told her that he thought that Noah would come here to finish his threat. The short time he'd known her told him that she wasn't the sort to tackle her problems head-on.

Officer Reading's comment returned to him. Kaylee had enough on her plate right now. He didn't need to add to it, even if he really believed that Noah hadn't fled south.

Or was he being selfish again, as Phoebe had so often accused him of being? Noah was his problem and standing here telling himself that Kaylee was in danger could be his own selfish way of foisting his problems onto her, of forcing her to help him.

Did he really believe that?

"Because why?"

With a blink, he brought her face back into focus. "You've gone through a lot. I was concerned about you."

An odd expression rolled over her features. Still, she said nothing. Just as he turned away, she stepped forward. "Eli?" Her voice had turned soft, hesitant.

He faced her. "Yes?"

Her throat bobbed and a small crease formed between her dark brows. "Did you call me last night?"

"No. Why?"

She shivered. The urge to hold her close swelled in him, but he pushed it away when she stepped back. "Why, Kaylee? Who called you?"

"I'm not sure. There was a moment of silence before the person hung up."

His heart skipped a beat. "Do you know what the number was?"

"No. I can't afford call display or even that last-number-dialed feature. It took me a long time to fall asleep." She paused. "There are some nuts out there who like to scare people just because they're bored in the evening. My boss said this area is bad for that. And it's not as if what happened to me is a secret. It was probably just kids."

Or it could be Noah, Eli thought.

Kaylee peered at him. Her hands had found each other, her fingers tightly intertwined. "I know what you're thinking. You think it was Noah. But he's headed south. He wouldn't leave his followers and risk them abandoning him."

She threw off the whole idea with a hasty shake of her head. "He wouldn't have stuck around. Look, I just don't want to deal with this!"

With one swift step, he hauled her to him. There was nothing he could do but let her sag in his arms. Should he be telling her that he believed it *was* Noah?

No. She'd run away. And without her as a lure, he'd lose his chance to stop Noah once and for all.

He shut his eyes. Phoebe was right. He *was* being selfish. He was only using the notion of waiting for his investigator's call as an excuse to hang around, all the while using Kaylee as bait.

His stomach twisted. Not the best way for a Christian to act. The old fears within him reared up, nasty and cold like the words Noah said once when they were reaching the end of their teenage years, when John, their second cousin, had sparked dangerous ideas inside of him. *"We're a lot alike, Eli."*

Just before that, Eli had told Noah he was nuts to think people would walk away from organized religion just because the world seemed headed for disaster.

Noah had smiled and repeated his comment, knowing it would push Eli's buttons. "We are alike, you and I. Only, I'm insightful and creative enough to make my own religion—a religion based on the truth of today, not old myths that have worn out their welcome."

Eli opened his eyes to see a close-up of Kaylee's dark, soft hair, each strand fine and wavy, its faint scent of apple shampoo teasing his nose.

He had to find Phoebe, save her from their brother, using everything God had given him. Including Kaylee?

With that resolution, he gripped her tighter and prayed silently.

"He's checked into the Valley View Motel up by the highway. It's quiet this time of year, so he's their only guest," Lois told Kaylee after supper that evening. She'd asked Kaylee over for tea before Kaylee had to return to the rec center. Jenn had asked her to lock up after the men's basketball game finished and Kaylee was free until then.

"Everyone in town knows he's here," Lois continued. "And why. He's here because of you."

With a flick of her gaze up to the older woman, Kaylee wrapped her hands around the mug of hot tea. Yes, Eli had said he was sticking around. She knew enough to guess his plan.

But she still didn't know what to make of his decision to stay. He'd been driven all these years to find Phoebe and free her. Why stop now?

Because of her? No. They'd only just met.

Because of Noah? Did he suspect he was here?

A cold shiver rippled through her and she lifted the steaming mug to swallow another sip. Eli was wrong.

"It was on the news last night, along with that tropical storm coming. I heard you could see the smoke from the explosion on the highway." Lois still chattered on. If she'd asked Kaylee here to glean some information on what had happened yesterday, she'd forgotten to ask the questions.

Kaylee looked up at the older woman. "I didn't watch the news."

Lois gave her a sympathetic smile. "I don't imagine."

"I wish it hadn't been reported."

"It'll be in the news for a while. They even have some kind of forensic bomb squad there trying to figure out what explosives were used, but it could take months, the reporter said. Bombs and explosions and such are a fact of life now, I'm afraid."

And with Noah having dropped out of sight, they'll never find him, Kaylee thought as Lois topped up her tea.

"They had the water bombers on standby, I heard," Lois added. "And when I found out it concerned the very compound where you were held, I paid attention. Did any reporters call you?"

Kaylee nodded. "A couple, but I said I didn't want to talk." It wasn't their calls that lingered in her mind. It was the other one.

"I should go," she said before gulping down her tea and pushing back her chair. "I have a few things to do at work while the men finish up their game." Her head was beginning to pound. The fresh, crisp air on the walk down to the rec center would do her good.

She paused. Should she be walking, alone, if Noah was out there? But Noah wasn't out there; he wouldn't leave his followers. They were too important to him and his need for control. She'd learned that the hard way.

Lois reached out and touched her hand and she started. "Oh, dear thing! This is my fault, isn't it?" The older woman bit her lip, looking as if she was ready to cry. "Honey, if I hadn't told you that story about my husband leaving for Korea, and that man helping us, you'd have never decided to go back to Maine with that Eli Nash and none of this would have happened!"

Kaylee looked over at her friend and saw the etched concern on her face that must have been a mirror of her own. Tears stung her eyes. Now Lois was feeling guilty, too? Were they all going to be prisoners of Noah Nash?

She leaned forward, her jaw tightening. "Lois, you did the right thing. Look, if we hadn't gone to that compound, those explosives may not have been found until some kids went there. Noah would have hurt or killed innocent teens backroading with four wheelers. You did the right thing, though you didn't realize it at the time. Noah's plans were thwarted."

And she wasn't going to be a prisoner to him, she added to herself. Forget it. She was free. And while that might get Noah Nash's goat, as her grandmother would say, she wasn't going to turn her life back into the fearful, captive one she'd had while in the compound.

Fear is the lack of trust. Noah had said that more than once.

As much as she hated to admit it, he was right. Fear *is* the lack of trust. But a trust in what, a part of her asked. Certainly not Noah.

With gritted teeth at the way he still ruled her, she rose and shoved her mug under the kitchen tap. Noah was wrong. Phoebe was wrong to believe him. Kaylee twisted off the faucet. And she was wrong to dwell on those people. They had destroyed her life and allowed Trisha to die.

She rinsed her mug out in the sink and set it on the rack to dry. Then, with as strong a smile as she could imagine, she said, "It's not your fault, Lois. I made the decision to help Eli. I'm not going to let Noah Nash win here. He's had enough influence over me to last a hundred lifetimes."

Lois nodded her approval. "That's my girl."

After giving the elderly woman a warm hug and Pepe a pat on the head, Kaylee walked out into the street. She wouldn't take her car. She'd tried it earlier and the rickety old thing barely turned over.

Autumn had turned the air crisp and sharp. The nice days would soon be over. Above, the clouds looked like chunks of ice floating in a dark liquid. Lois had said a tropical storm was on its way, up from the deep south. The warm temperature might be welcome, but after the wet summer they'd had, the rainfall wouldn't be.

She pulled up her zipper so the cool breeze from the Saint John River wouldn't trickle down her neck. She'd been cold enough for the last few years.

At the end of her cul-de-sac, she paused. Then turned around. The street lay silently, chillingly before her.

A tingle on the back of her neck whispered that someone was watching her.

SEVEN

Pray constantly. Give thanks in all circumstances. Lois had said they were Pastor Paul's favorite Bible words, but that even he admitted it was hard to do. Kaylee's steps faltered. God felt too far away to reach by a simple prayer.

How was she supposed to pray and give thanks when the night crawled over her like this?

She spun and returned to her walk, her pace faster than before. The rec center was less than five minutes away. Behind her, a dog barked. From the sound of the high-pitched yip, it had to be Lois's dog.

The tingling in her neck continued. The agitated barking echoed through the streets.

Ahead, where the street she was hurrying down met River Road, a figure stepped out from a dark corner and turned to her.

Her heart stalled and her steps faltered. *Noah.*

No, she wouldn't be fooled again. The short hair and wary bearing belonged to Eli, not his brother.

She sagged. Quickening her steps, she hurried toward him. As soon as she reached him, the dog stopped its incessant barking.

"What are you doing out so late?" she asked. "I mean, I'm due to lock up the gym when the men finish their basketball game or else I'd be asleep by now."

"Why didn't you drive down?"

"I don't want to waste the gas and wear and tear on my car. It's old and rickety enough as it is and it's been hard to start today for some reason." She kept on walking. Eli, however, stood and stared up the street toward her cul-de-sac. She hesitated a few yards away. "What's wrong?"

"Nothing." He threw one last glance over his shoulder and strode toward her. "Let me help you lock up. Then I'll walk you home."

"Thank you." She couldn't deny her relief at his suggestion. Tonight the streets felt sinister.

They walked the rest of the short distance in silence, down into the dip on the River Road, then up past the narrow park that lay to their left. Inside the rec center, she waved to one man who'd taken a break outside the gym for a quick swig of water.

"Hi, Paul," she said.

"Hey, Kaylee, come to lock up? Or are you here to watch my team win?" He chuckled, but then stopped abruptly when he saw Eli at the door.

She hastily introduced the men. Pastor Paul Riggs did a lot of outreach, his specialty was using sports. The two men sized each other up, then her pastor reached out to pump Eli's hand. They spoke briefly before Pastor Paul threw his empty water bottle back into his bag.

"You look good, Kaylee," he said, wiping his forehead with the short sleeve of his shirt. "I think Lois's cooking is putting some meat on you." He smiled at them and headed back into the gym.

"Are you?"

She blinked at Eli. "Putting on weight? A bit. I didn't think it would be so hard."

"It's the stress. Give it time. Plus, you didn't eat right for two years."

She stooped to pick up a discarded candy wrapper. It was from the store beside the gym, a product made right on the premises. "No, we didn't," she said, tossing the wrapper into the garbage can nearby. "Some fresh vegetables when they ripened in the garden and then mostly rice and pasta in the winter. There just wasn't very much to go around."

Eli's expression darkened. "You had no meat or milk? No bread?"

"No. The children got powdered milk, but meat only came when a chicken died. We had tea, but no sugar for it." Her stomach ached, ripping away any appetite she may have had for an evening snack. No wonder she was still too skinny.

Eli folded his arms, his brows meeting and his mouth tight.

She watched the game through the protected window. "I remember one day this past spring, when Noah and the men took some of the women to get groceries and seeds, that we had nothing to eat, those of us who were left. I think the ones who went shopping also went to a restaurant."

"What's wrong with that?"

"Nothing I suppose. It's just that we had no food in the house. We'd been eating sparsely for weeks and it was taking its toll on us. Anyway, one of the women had reached the end of her rope. The children, there were three with us, were irritable and hungry.

The woman went outside and collected lamb's-quarter."

"What's that?"

"It's that plant that has pointed leaves and some kind of silvery dust on its new sprouts. It grows the fastest in early spring. But it cooks up like young spinach, only not as strong tasting. Oh, it was good. Delicious. Even the kids ate and ate."

He tilted his head. "Why are you sad about that? As far as I can tell, getting kids to eat any vegetables is a good thing."

She smiled briefly and shrugged. "In that way, yes, it was good. But when the others came home, Phoebe found out about it from one of the kids. She told Noah." Her gaze clouded and she flicked her head away from him. "The woman who picked and cooked the lamb's-quarter for us was punished."

She bustled into the office, knowing Eli would follow her. "I shouldn't have brought it up. It's just that..."

Eli straightened. "That what? That the woman did the right thing?"

She couldn't look at him. "Noah didn't want us to eat it because he said it represented the evil that lured us away from the truth. The lust for food was the same as the lust for the evils around us." She lifted her hand. "It was just another way he controlled us, I know that now. But that day...we were starving. So we picked bowls and bowls of it. It felt so good to eat it."

"What was wrong with that?"

She could still taste the fresh flavor, the little bit of salt and pepper they'd dared to sprinkle on it. The lure of fresh food had been powerful. "I remember wondering if Noah had been right."

"About what?"

"About the lamb's-quarter. With a craving that strong, it had almost felt sinful to eat it, to want it so much, you'd give anything for it. Noah quoted the story of how Esau sold his birthright for a bowl of stew."

Eli bent his head down and lifted her chin with his finger. That little touch felt so comforting. "Don't let Noah twist the Bible to suit himself. Yes, Esau sold his birthright to Jacob, because he cared only for his own immediate needs. He showed lack of faith. I don't see you in that same way."

She shut her eyes, confusion swirling around her at Eli's intuition. She didn't need to be a psychologist to see that he was as smooth a talker as his brother was. "Noah was determined that the woman be purged of evil."

With an abrupt shiver, she stepped away from him. "I don't want to talk about it anymore. I remember feeling so guilty that we'd eaten those greens. I even prayed about it. Noah could be so persuasive and dangerous, and when I realized that I was actually starting to believe him about some things, it scared me. I was thinking about that incident just before I decided to escape." She folded her arms to hug herself.

Eli took her arms and set them down at her sides. "Don't feel guilty. And don't fight the need to talk this out."

"Who wants to rehash everything?" she whispered, not meeting his gaze, but rather turning to watch out the caged window at the basketball game as it came to a close.

He didn't answer her question. Rather, he leaned back against the wall. She could hear the men in the gym cheering and yelling and shaking hands. They'd soon pour out the door beside her, grab their packs and bags and leave. Eli would take her home and she'd be alone again for another night.

Did that bother her?

"It helps to tackle issues head on," Eli answered with a soft voice. "It robs them of their power over you. Don't think it was your fault that he was starting to sway you. He's manipulative and starvation is a form of control. But you saw what was happening and got out. That's what counts."

"I guess so." She wanted to walk into Eli's arms again. She wanted to feel the comfort and protection she knew she'd find there.

But she didn't know him very well, though she did know he was driven, like his brother.

What if he turned out to be as dangerous as Noah? What if she was replacing one persuasive man with another?

The door to the gym flew open and the men spilled out. Kaylee peeked out of the office to watch them all gather up their jackets and gym bags and filter into the night.

Only Pastor Paul remained. Still out of breath, he grinned at her. "Do you need a drive home, Kaylee? I'm taking some of the guys that way."

"I'll take her home."

Paul looked at Eli's determined expression then nodded. He turned to Kaylee. "Are you working tomorrow night? We could use a hand with the youth group's floor-hockey game. My usual assistants are university students, but they're all studying. Exams are coming up."

He'd been trying to get her involved in the church. She'd resisted so far, begging off due to fatigue. She hesitated.

Paul leaned forward to smile encouragingly. "It's for the kids. To keep them off the streets." He looked at his watch. "Gotta go. I'll see you at six tomorrow night?"

"Okay." Kaylee found herself smiling. "As long as they don't wear me out."

"Sorry. No guarantees on that," Paul answered cheerfully, slinging his gym bag over his shoulder. "They wear out everyone who's more than twenty-one. That's why we need help. Tag-team monitoring."

He threw a speculative look at Eli. "If you're sticking around, you're welcome to come, too. We're having sundaes after."

"If Kaylee's going, I'll be there."

Paul lifted his eyebrows as they all turned to leave. Like a good minister, Paul had a gregarious personality *and* tact. But he wasn't naive. He was a man, too. Did that mean he trusted Eli or not?

The building now locked up, she and Eli fell into step along the sidewalk. The clouds had moved in and Kaylee felt a warm, southerly breeze rise. Lois's prediction on that tropical storm was coming true.

As they reached the street where they'd met, the dog in the distance began to bark again. The same frenzied barking as before.

"Is that Pepe?" Eli asked as they walked.

"I don't know." She started to laugh softly. "If it is him, maybe I should start to feed him like the previous tenants did. Maybe that's all he wants."

"He sounds more agitated than hungry."

As they stepped off the sidewalk to meet Kaylee's cul-de-sac, the dog let out a short yelp.

Followed by a skin-prickling silence.

EIGHT

"Kaylee's neighbor, Lois Smith, found him this morning. Poor thing probably died in the night. Before she went to bed, she noticed the broken chain. She figured he'd decided to take off for a run. He's done that before."

Eli could barely hear Paul Riggs' voice over the din of teenagers playing floor hockey. "Lois was pretty upset. She called the police immediately because she knew her nephew was working. He answered the call."

They stood in one corner. A whistle dangled around Paul's neck, while Eli held the stopwatch. The two men had decided on two five-minute scrimmages, junior youth against the senior youth. It looked as if the juniors were going to win but, frankly, Eli wasn't watching the timer in his hand. He scanned the gym for Kaylee and found her across the floor, ducking the small white ball as it whipped past her. She barely escaped being sandwiched between two boys as they fought for possession.

"Big dog?" he asked Paul.

"Not really. I remember when I first visited Lois. He was just an average-sized brown mutt with an an-

noying high-pitched bark. He was okay once he got to sniff you, but overall, I'd say he was just a chicken in a dog's body."

"Does this sort of thing happen a lot here?"

Paul shook his head. "I've never heard of it, and I've lived here for almost a decade."

"That dog *was* upset last night. Kaylee said Lois doesn't always hear it."

"I'm not surprised. She cranks her TV up because she's half-deaf. Won't admit it, though. Jim Reading phoned me, thinking Lois might appreciate a visit after what happened. When I called her this afternoon, she said she thought a bear might have wandered into the village."

Eli shook his head. "Black bears are apt to leave a potent smell wherever they go. I don't remember smelling that last night."

Paul lifted his whistle, then stopped. "How do you know about bears?"

"I'm from rural New York state. Where we lived, we had black bears. Last night, there was no garbage out and most bears would have headed toward downtown to search through the restaurant's garbage there. Were there any reports of a bear?"

Shaking his head, Paul blew his whistle at some infraction. After a moment, the play resumed and he returned to stand beside Eli. "Actually, you're right to be suspicious. The police think it's foul play. Someone, not something, killed that dog."

"To shut it up?"

"My thoughts exactly." Paul blew the whistle again and shouted out that the time had expired. Eli hadn't even thought to look down at the stopwatch in his palm.

To shut the dog up? Cold rippled down his back. He leaned slightly toward the pastor. "Did you tell Kaylee?"

"No. We were so busy picking up the kids and getting ready for youth group." Paul's expression turned intense. "And I told Lois not to, either. At least not right away. She doesn't need the worry. But this is a small town. She's bound to find out."

Not if he had something to do with it, Eli vowed. He should check out Kaylee's backyard, anyway. Noah was good at hiding in difficult places, but Eli hadn't spent all that time working with the police without picking up a few tricks himself. If Noah had been in her backyard, he would find evidence of it. Noah was a good outdoorsman, knowing how to hide his presence, but Eli was good, too.

"Do you know something about this?"

He looked up at Paul's frown. "No. After Kaylee locked up and we started walking, we heard a dog cry out and then there was nothing. We didn't know whose dog it was."

Paul shook his head. "As soon as my wife found out, she decided to keep our dog in. She thinks it was a burglar."

Eli said nothing.

The rest of the evening was wild, chaotic and typically teen-oriented. Finally, near nine o'clock, the teens had all headed home. By nine-thirty, with Kaylee and Eli to help, the gym, kitchen and lounge were all tidied up.

Paul killed the lights to the gym as they all left. "Thanks, you two. I don't know what I would have done if I had to look after these kids alone. Will I see you both at church on Sunday?"

"Yes," Eli answered automatically. Then, catching

a glimpse of Kaylee's tired, doelike expression as she walked past him, contrition swept over him.

He needed to hear from his investigator. And soon.

Sunday morning the church parking lot was full. Eli found a spot at the far corner and as he walked around to open the door for Kaylee, he nodded to an older couple parking near them. Above, the sky seemed as dark as a winter dusk. That tropical storm was due today.

Kaylee climbed out of his car and followed his glance up at the darkening sky. "I'm glad I didn't bring my car. With the wet weather due, it may not start."

"What exactly is the car doing?"

"Not starting. It was fine a week ago, but now, it barely cranks. Sometimes all I get is a clicking noise."

"Your battery is dying. It sounds like you don't have enough juice to turn over the engine."

"Great. I can't afford a new battery. Good thing I live walking distance to work."

"Maybe it only needs to be charged. I'll have a look at it, if you'd like?"

She smiled a thank-you at him as they made their way into the sanctuary. The early service attracted quite a few. The people here all had nice, ordered lives. They worked during the week and fellowshipped on Sunday. He swallowed. His life was too itinerant and it wouldn't change until he freed Phoebe.

And what about Kaylee? There she was, trying her best to lead a normal life after all Noah had done. Her disgust for him and his cult members was more than obvious and included Phoebe. To her, Phoebe was as responsible for Trisha's death as Noah was. She

wanted to cut them all loose from her memories and start her life again. He was a living, breathing reminder to her.

Kaylee spotted Lois with another elderly woman. Both scooted over to let her and Eli into the pew.

Kaylee chuckled. "All the little old ladies take up these seats in the back. I think they like to watch the congregation come in."

"No, it's not that," Lois beside her stated in a tart tone. "Most of them need hearing aids and use the earphones from the sound system. You have to sit in the back for them. I don't need one, mind you, but these ladies are my friends."

Kaylee winked at him before leaning close enough for her low whisper to be heard only by him. "I was expecting Lois to be a bit more pleased I was here, but she seems a bit cranky. I think she's starting to realize *she* needs a hearing aid." With a light shrug, she settled back in the pew.

He smiled briefly, grateful for her relaxed mood. Obviously, Lois hadn't told her about Pepe. But from the woman's behavior, his death bothered her very much.

The service was short, full of prayer, which allowed Eli's thoughts to wander to Kaylee. She was a mix of contradictions. Trying to start her life over, oddly serene here in church and yet still wracked with guilt for the things she'd said and done.

She believed God was punishing her for being swayed by Noah and beginning to believe his warped philosophies.

How could she really believe that because she'd been forced to say blasphemous words for Noah, the Lord would never forgive her?

Or was it in part humiliation she felt? To believe a man, only to have him kill her beloved sister?

Eli didn't know her well enough to guess.

But, he realized with growing concern, he *wanted* to know her that well.

The service ended and after attending the adult Sunday school, Eli and Kaylee returned to the sanctuary for the regular service.

"I told you so," she whispered with a snicker as they walked up the center aisle, past the back pews now filled with elderly ladies. "All the old ladies take the back seats."

Eli smiled and nodded back, but he felt his smile quickly drift away. All that had happened still disturbed him. He only half listened to the message and struggled through the prayers, trying to stay focused.

"What's wrong?" she asked as the service ended and people began to filter out.

What could he say? That he believed his insane brother was hanging around? For the first time in years, she felt safe. Who was he to rob her of that on a suspicion he couldn't confirm?

And being here was by her good graces. He'd seen Officer Reading eyeing him from across the aisle. Kaylee would only have to say one word to the man and he'd be asked to leave town.

Yet, if he told her what he suspected, she'd most likely take off, probably go home. On the surface, it sounded like a good idea, but what about Noah? What would he do?

And he suspected that Kaylee was closer to leaving than she appeared. She had friends and an aunt in Nova Scotia, people in her hometown that cared for her. He'd heard her talking about them to one of the other parishioners, admitting that it was past time to visit them.

"Hello again!" A voice blasted out from behind him. Eli turned. A tall, thin man with a shock of white hair and a ready smile grabbed his hand and pumped it. "Good to see you here. Did you find the provincial walking trail? You really can't miss it."

Confused a moment, Eli frowned. "I'm sorry, do I know you?"

"Well, we haven't been formally introduced. I'm Hec Haines."

Eli peered at the man, still unsure why he'd asked about the trail. "I'm Eli Nash. I'm staying up—"

"Yes, up at the motel. You told me."

"I did?"

"Yesterday. So, did you find the trail?"

Eli felt his frown deepen. "I didn't ask for directions to the trail yesterday." Kaylee had told him flat-out that she was planning to sleep in and then do housework all day. He'd taken the opportunity to sleep in himself. The only time he'd been out was for a short drive to the local deli.

"Of course you didn't *ask* for directions. I offered them. You were looking for a shortcut through town."

Eli watched Kaylee assist an elderly lady out of the last pew. She was well out of earshot. "When?" he asked.

"Thursday night, late. My dog's getting old and she has to go out at the oddest times. It had started to warm up with that storm on its way, so I didn't mind as much. Hate going out in the winter. But then again, I think I told you that."

Eli straightened and walked out of the pew. "I think you have me…"

Oh. His stomach flipped. He'd been halfway out when he turned back to stare at the man. Someone who looked like him was in town….

Noah.

NINE

"I know I'm not mistaking you for someone else, if that's what you're going to say. Not too many men your size around here with that blond of hair." The man peered at his head. "Mind you, did you get it cut? I thought it was a bit longer."

Eli swallowed. "How much longer?"

"Not much. A little bit." The man frowned. "I was sure it was you I spoke to. I don't usually forget a face. Terrible with names. What did you say yours was?"

"Eli Nash."

Hec's face lit up and he nodded vigorously. "Yes, yes, of course. That's what I thought you'd said. Sorry I didn't get a chance to introduce myself, but the dog was pretty excited."

Eli started. "Did your dog get upset?"

"Yes! You remember! Sorry about that. Sheba usually likes everyone. I don't know what got into her. She was quite snappy at you. She must not have liked the smell of your clothes. Very odd, indeed."

"I hope she's better now," Eli murmured.

"Oh, she was fine after you left. Crazy old dog. Maybe she's getting senile. After you mentioned that

I would definitely be seeing you again, she just let loose, didn't she?"

Eli stared at the man. "I don't remember. I'm sorry." His heart pounded hard in his chest and he could feel the blood draining from his face.

"Oh, nothing to be sorry about. I feel badly that she acted so nasty. But you probably made it worse by laughing at her."

Laughing? "Um, that was rude of me. I don't know what to say." He didn't. He had no desire to tell this man someone had impersonated him. The guy probably wouldn't believe him, anyway.

"Don't worry about it. I'm just glad you were able to make it to church today. We talked about you coming here. Well, only briefly. I had to keep Sheba away from you."

Eli could hardly breathe. Laughing at an animal, telling a perfect stranger you'd see him again. Ice raced down his spine, delivering a harsh shiver.

"What exactly did he, I mean, I say to you? I'm sorry if I don't recall the conversation."

Hec drummed his fingers along the back of the pew. "Not much. Just that you'd planned to go to church. Oh, yes, also something about you being predictable when it comes to Sundays."

Eli scowled.

As if he felt he'd made a faux pas, Hec hastily glanced over his shoulder. "Well, coffee's ready. How's about a cup? We usually fellowship after the service."

"Thank you. I could use a cup." Eli followed the man out. If truth be told, he could use way more than a cup of coffee right now. He could feel sweat breaking out on his forehead.

Was it Noah who'd met with Hec? In the darkness, he and his brother could pass for twins. Only the dog got a sense of Noah's true nature.

Had Noah cut his hair to pass himself off as Eli? Was it possible?

Yes. More than possible, it was downright probable. And knowing Eli would come to church, Noah had grasped the opportunity to send him a message.

I'm here. And people think I'm you.

Kaylee spotted him and smiled before turning her attention back to the older lady she'd helped. She was lovely, her dark hair dancing as she laughed at something the elderly lady said.

A surge of emotion swelled in his throat. She was so oblivious to any danger. And so much in denial. He should tell her. He could make her believe him, but it would send her flying from here.

That would keep her safe, right?

Maybe, maybe not.

What it wouldn't do was get him closer to Noah. Or Phoebe.

And, he told himself, above everything else, he needed to find Phoebe.

He'd given up everything to find her. He owed it to his parents. They were the ones who'd missed her the most.

Finding and freeing Phoebe would be a big blow to Noah's control over his cult. With his most ardent follower gone, the rest would really be lost sheep and Noah might be forced to give up this little game.

Eli walked slowly up the center aisle toward Kaylee. He had to find Phoebe.

But with Noah out there impersonating him, would finding Phoebe be at Kaylee's expense?

Kaylee was nearly dead and desperately needed to go home. Friday night had really drained her, and though she'd spent Saturday resting, exhaustion still lingered heavily. Her doctor had told her that she'd lost a lot of muscle and would tire easily, but it hadn't been until she tried to get out of bed Sunday morning that she really believed him.

Now, as she hung on to the chair she'd snagged for Lois, who had looked as if she wasn't feeling well herself, Kaylee noticed Eli making his way to her after talking to Hec Haines. His eyebrows had knitted together and a grim line replaced his mouth. What was the matter? Had he noticed her fatigue, too?

"Ready?" he asked.

"Yes. I'm absolutely wiped. I was just about to tell Lois not to bother making any tea for me this afternoon, but she's left with one of the other ladies. They must be going out to lunch." She frowned. "She usually has me over."

"You can see her later. Let's go." He took her arm with his left hand and thrust open the vestry door with his right.

She threw him a curious look as they weaved through the parked cars toward his. First Lois was acting somewhat short and now Eli was acting as if church was the last place he wanted to be. Had he realized he was losing valuable time here, when he should be heading south?

Did she want him to go?

She refused to answer her own question, choosing

instead to study his chiseled features. More refined than Noah's, Eli's face bore a warm concern. She let her gaze drift down, along the strong arms and out to his long, tanned fingers.

Why was he here, wasting his time and probably his hard-earned money? Surely not for her?

She climbed wearily into the passenger seat of his car. "Oh, dear, I forgot my paycheck at work. I don't feel like it, but I should stop by and pick it up."

With a nod, he swung the car around. Minutes later, as they entered the rec center's office, she stifled a yawn. "Sorry. I really *am* tired."

"You can rest when you get home."

"Yes, I will." She sniffed the air. "It smells funny in here."

Eli inhaled. "I smell candy." He sniffed again. "Maybe from that candy store? They must be making a batch of candy."

"It's strong today."

Nodding, Eli scanned the office. She found her own eyes roaming over the desks and chairs and counters.

Several candy wrappers were tossed aimlessly on the floor in front of Jenn's desk. She must have called in a few kids to read them the riot act for kicking volleyballs. A big no-no in her books.

Kaylee walked over to the mail slots at the far side. Among the pigeonholes was one for items such as scissors and rulers and a magnifying glass because Jenn claimed she wasn't paid enough to buy reading glasses.

The bright blue scissors that always caught her eyes were gone. She turned, skimming each desk and the credenza. They must be away in a drawer.

"What's wrong? Your check isn't there?"

"No." Absently, she drew out her envelope and waved it. "But the scissors are gone. Jenn must have moved them."

"Do you need them?"

She cleared her throat. "My fingernails are too short to open the envelope. Phoebe was in charge of making sure all the women's nails were trimmed, not that we were healthy enough to grow them in the first place."

When she noticed his darkening look, she added, "The doctor said they'll grow back, but it may take several months and I'll probably see a ridge in them when they do. As a result, I've taken to using the scissors to open envelopes."

Eli looked around, then bent over to scoop up some candy wrappers. He dropped them into the wastebasket beside the desk. "I wouldn't be surprised if Jenn's hid them away. Kids have a habit of 'borrowing' things."

"That's a possibility. The kids aren't supposed to come in here, but Jenn is usually alone in the office, so if she had to leave..." She shoved her paycheck in her small knapsack and walked into the corridor. "I'll open it at home. It's no big deal." She let out a derisive noise. "The most exciting part of my afternoon is reading my paycheck."

Eli followed her out, shutting off the light and closing the door behind him. She watched him. The smell of candy remained stronger out there, the corridor being closer to the shop next door.

Kaylee locked up in silence. The moment she was done, Eli took her hand to study her short, well-filed fingernails. She tugged back her hand, hating the way her fingers looked.

Eli dropped his arm. "It's a wonder he didn't cut your hair."

"He seemed to favor long hair. He had his long enough."

Without warning, he wove his fingers through her hair and allowed the strands to slide free. Her breath stalled in her lungs as he spoke. "You have beautiful hair, even after being malnourished."

Then, as suddenly as he'd fingered her hair, he shoved his hands into his pockets. "I'd like to see it in a year."

Would you? Are you planning to stay that long? Or are you coming back?

She dropped the internal questions as soon as they arrived. The sooner she was done with the Nash siblings, the sooner she'd be able to get her life back on track.

On track to where? Since meeting Eli, she'd never felt so…at loose ends.

At home, after a quick bite to eat, she lay down on the couch. To her surprise, she awoke to find night already settling on her house.

The wind rattled the siding outside. Her house stood high on a knoll and her backyard dipped dramatically into the ravine that arced around the cul-de-sac before making its way down to the river. When coming from the south, as it was doing now, the wind found little opposition until it hit her house. The Saint John River valley acted like a wind tunnel, with her house a block through the middle of it.

Wearily, Kaylee rose. She hadn't planned to sleep so long. A quick check of the time on the wall clock told her that she'd slept past five. A glance outside on her way to the kitchen told her that a thick blanket of clouds aided the early dusk.

She grabbed some bread, preparing to make a sandwich for herself but stopped at the sink. The kitchen window looked out onto her back deck. She looked forward to next summer when she could sit out there and enjoy the warm sun.

A flicker of bright red danced upward in the breeze. Kaylee stretched up on tiptoes. The wind drove it down and then up, a flashing dance around the wood rails.

Curious, she walked to the sliding door. Finding a break in the clouds, the sun made one last attempt to shine. A single yellow ray struck the house.

The red fluttered again. A ribbon? No, a leash. Lois's dog leash?

Kaylee stepped onto the deck. The wind buffeted her. She grabbed the leash and tugged, but it had wrapped itself around the rails.

Stooping, she began to untangle it, only to find the knot tighter than she expected.

Something moved under her. Under the deck. She froze. Then, in a moment of bravery that seemed to come from nowhere, she called out, "Eli?"

A familiar voice answered her. "Hello, Kaylee. It's me."

TEN

Eli stepped out from under the deck.

She sighed, sagging enough to feel relief turn her bones to jelly. Her hand went to her heart. "You scared me! I didn't know *what* was underneath."

The sun relented in its fight against the storm and the yard around them dulled into windy darkness.

"Sorry."

"Why are you here?"

"To keep an eye on you." Evenly, he surveyed the short backyard, especially where the drop off to the ravine began. "And to check the area out."

She bit her lip. To keep an eye on her? For how long?

Her heartbeat bumped up a notch. "Is everything all right?" She wanted to ask him what he meant by his words, but what if he wasn't staying? What if this was the last time she'd see him?

Disappointment caught in her throat, but she forced it down again. He was itinerant and Phoebe needed him. She didn't.

She toyed with the idea of inviting him for supper, but held back. With just a minimum-wage job, she had very little in her house to feed him. She didn't even have enough money to order in pizza.

Not a good idea, anyway, whether or not he was leaving Riverline.

She grabbed the leash still tangled around the wood. "Help me with this leash. It must belong to Lois's dog. I'll give it to her tomorrow."

Without speaking, Eli stepped closer to the deck and began to untangle the leash. She watched the cuff of his jacket catch slightly on the wood. Uncertainty floated through her as she looked down through the deck boards at him. The sun tried one more brief attempt to break up the clouds and in that moment, the yellow rays turned Eli's skin a pale color. Pale like Noah usually was, made worse by the faded blue jacket. Eli was more tanned, no doubt spending more time outside than his brother did. The weak fall sun, however, wasn't doing him the justice he deserved.

She should really offer him something, she thought as he reached through the deck to pass her the leash.

Maybe just a cup of coffee?

She stooped to take the leash and their fingers brushed at the tips. She pulled hers back, feeling foolish that she'd even noticed it. "Would you like to come in for a cup of coffee?"

The sun retreated behind a bank of rain-laden clouds. The only light came from the kitchen, now casting a dull glow onto them. She waited for his answer.

A small smile tugged at his mouth, nothing like she'd seen before. So like Noah's she had to shake off the mental image. "Would that really be a good idea?"

"It would only be a coffee. I know you want to maintain a certain decorum. Pastor Paul talks about that sometimes, but surely you can spend *some* time alone with a woman."

He laughed and tilted his head down. She couldn't see the expression well, especially in the encroaching darkness.

He shook his head. "Kaylee, all men are alike. Never forget that. We have our own individual standards, yes, but inside, we're all the same."

"You're not the same as Noah!"

"We're more alike than you realize. Growing up together, it wasn't hard to see we were cut from the same cloth, as my grandmother used to say." His smile drifted off. "She didn't like Noah, said he was bad. But she liked me. Said I wasn't the same."

"You aren't."

"No. I *am* the same as he is. Saved, yes, but always one step from sliding into the evil that *is* Noah. Always remember that, Kaylee."

He looked up at her and a shiver danced down her spine. So like Noah. And yet, here was Eli, the kinder, gentler brother, warning her that he was just as bad as his brother was. That kind of honesty was touching.

And true, maybe? Was she getting involved with a man who was so much like the very man who'd killed her sister?

The wind slid across him and up toward her as she remained bent down. She caught the sweet scent of gum or candy. And something else, too. The smell of cooked eggs, or matches just lit? What was it?

A strange mix of smells, it was. Sweet and yet acrid.

But the sweet smell was by far stronger. Was he chewing a fresh stick of gum?

Having caught that smell, her stomach growled.

She shut her eyes briefly. She hadn't had the stomach for junk food lately and her doctor had advised against it, but now that Eli had some…

When she opened her eyes again, he was gone.

Unnerved, Kaylee straightened slowly, the leash still dangling in her hand. The wind, supposedly warm according to the forecast, turned suddenly cold.

"Eli?"

No answer. He was gone without a goodbye. Was this for good? She hated that she didn't know him well enough to make an educated guess.

Maybe it was best that he declined her offer to come inside. If she got involved with him, what kind of future would she have? He only wanted one thing.

And Eli had just warned her that he was as dangerous as Noah was, too. How easy would it be for her to become involved with Eli? Too easy. She'd listen to him, understand him. Be influenced by him.

She shivered and the sting of tears began again. No. Go inside. Forget them both, especially Eli.

Hastily, she retreated inside, where the small supper of a sandwich and some raw carrots waited to be prepared. She should eat. Yet she knew it was going to sit hollowly inside of her.

The rain began overnight. Kaylee awoke early to the heavy drum of it. The house creaked and groaned from the wind. It wasn't going to be a good walk down to the gym. And with this dampness, she didn't dare take the car and have the temperamental thing quit while she was going downhill in the rain.

The phone rang, causing her to jolt. She threw off the covers and hurried into the living room to answer it. "Hello?"

"It's me, Jenn. I cancelled all the activities because of the rain. But I'd still like you to come in this evening to clean. I hear the rain's supposed to let up by then or at least taper off. I've put a new box of detergent by the washer. We went through the last one pretty fast, but I need you to wash the jerseys. By the way, our dryer is acting up again. We're supposed to get a new one. Be careful."

Kaylee stifled a yawn. A day at home sounded good to her. "Thank you."

"Hey, maybe you can get that new boyfriend of yours to come in with you," Jenn teased.

"He's not my boyfriend." She cringed when she heard the chill in her voice.

Jenn seemed unaffected. "Not yet. But I'd say that could change. He's been making himself well known around here."

The wind slashed rain against the sliding door to the deck. Jenn let out a soft, disapproving snort. "Listen to that gust! I should go. I have a few more calls to make. Come in around five, okay?" She laughed. "And don't forget your rubber boots, girl. You're going to need them for the walk down here."

"I imagine." Hopefully, she thought, the weather will have calmed down by the time she had to leave for work.

The rain had eased, but the wind continued, shoving Kaylee down the hill toward the river. Temporary barricades warned people away from the low spots on the roads and she automatically avoided the narrow park that skirted the now fast-flowing river. Not a single soul was out, not even the curious teenagers who might defy parents' orders to see the storm damage firsthand. A sense of waiting had descended on the downtown area.

When she reached the gym, she saw Eli pull into one of the many vacant parking spots. "I stopped by your house," he said as he strode toward her. "I was hoping to take you to work."

He hadn't left. Elation plowed through her, and she found herself grinning foolishly. "No need. I had that gale to carry me down the hill," she said, flicking her head toward the west. "But a ride home would be welcomed."

"Uphill and against the wind, huh? I wouldn't want to battle it." He grinned back, so differently than the brief humorless smile he'd given her in her backyard last night. That one had felt almost smug. "I wouldn't want you to end up in the river."

She unlocked the door and walked inside, heading straight to the gym to survey how much cleaning she needed to do.

A layer of rainwater spread across the length of hardwood floor. She groaned. "Speaking of rivers."

Eli came up close behind her. "Where's it coming from?"

"The back emergency door. Thankfully, Jenn had this floor resealed this spring, but I'm still not sure that this won't do a load of damage."

"We'll have to push it back out and keep it from returning."

"Then out the side door would be best. It can drain over to the road and down the storm drains." They walked around to it. As soon as she opened it, the wind blasted rain into the gym.

Pulling up the hood on his jacket, Eli dove out into the storm. "Where are the sandbags?" he yelled, pointing to the edge of the playground where the trees met the grass. "Over in that shed back there?"

Kaylee shook her head as she peered out. "No, that's not used anymore. The sandbags should be lined up along the back wall. They're going to be heavy. I'll help you."

"No. You start pushing this flood toward this door. I'll manage."

She sighed. So true. As much as she hated to admit it, the strength she had years ago was gone. She'd be more of a hindrance than a help. "Okay. We have a mop somewhere. I'll go find it." She shook her head, then threw Eli an apologetic look. "This is going to take a while. You don't have to stick around. I'll call in Jenn."

Still outside, he put his back to the wind. "It's all right. I want to help. You'll need the muscle, even after Jenn gets here."

She smiled. "Thanks. There should be at least thirty sandbags out there. The town uses them to hold down the tent they have for summer camp. Perhaps you can dam up whatever is causing this leak."

"I'll redirect it toward the road. You find the mops."

Kaylee hurried down to the cleaner's room, detouring through the women's change room to grab the towel she kept in her locker. There weren't many janitor supplies for the building—Jenn had allergies—but the cleaner's room was big and held the washer and dryer used for sports clothing. Located in the older part of the center, it had a constant smell of old, stale sweat that Kaylee hadn't yet been able to remove.

She flicked the light switch, but the room remained

dark. With a quick glare at the burned-out bulb, she pushed the door open farther.

In the dim light, she located the mops, tucked in behind the dryer. "I found them!" she called over her shoulder, despite knowing that Eli probably wouldn't hear her.

"Ow!" In the dimness, she hit the dryer base with her boot. Her rubber boots were secondhand and donated, not to mention slightly small for her feet. She smacked the base of the old machine with snug and pinched toes, and it hurt.

Why on earth was the dryer sticking out so far? Someone must have been cleaning behind it. Jenn was always after the town to replace it. They must have relented.

She leaned forward, pressing her knee against the partially open door of the dryer, all the while reaching for the mop behind it.

Something snapped at her leg. In the dimness, she caught sight of a brilliant blue arc of electricity, just as it spiked again, a jagged bolt too bright and too painful to ignore.

She stumbled backward, slipped in the puddle she'd made with her boots and fell.

Automatically, she reached for something to grab, anything to catch her before she fell to the hard cement floor.

Without thinking, she chose the dryer door.

Another bolt crackled across to her hand. Fiery pain shot up her arm and she felt her body jerk and jerk again, backward or forward, she wasn't sure.

She felt the smack of cement against the back of her head.

Nothingness. Then, as she sucked in a needy lungful of air, she came alert with a start.

Her whole body ached. Her head throbbed hard, and when she tried to sit up, putting her hand to the slippery floor, she fell back again.

She let out a cry, half in pain and half in panic at the horror of what had happened.

She'd been electrocuted! Was she going to die? Alone, here?

Her legs shook, her arms had turned to jelly and sweat broke out on her face and back. She struggled to sit up, but just couldn't do it.

Her whole body ached.

"Eli!" she coughed out. "Eli!"

No answer. She called again. But already her throat refused to work, her vocal cords locked in some kind of tight, shock-induced spasm of their own.

Her head swam and throbbed. Even in the half dark, she felt the room spin around her.

She sank, crumbling at the base of door.

Her thoughts battled the fog in her brain. Confusion swirled in. She was alive. She should be able to stand, right?

But her muscles refused to work. Her head pounded more, stopping another attempt.

"Eli!" she tried again. Her throat felt as if she'd swallowed a thousand needles. Panic swept through her.

When she cried out one more time, she could barely hear herself. How would Eli hear her? He was outside, dragging and stacking sandbags in the middle of a storm. The remnants of a hurricane, no less. He'd never hear her over the wind.

With a frustratingly weak smack of her hand against the cement floor, she dropped her head and felt the dizziness overwhelm her.

ELEVEN

The lights flickered, then returned. Eli knew he should hurry before the power went off completely. Just as he set one of the last sandbags down, a noise cut weakly through the rain and wind.

What was that? He paused, the last sandbag in his hands, his head cocked to listen against the sounds of the storm. He'd taken longer than he thought. Someone had moved the sandbags, causing the eavestrough's downspout to direct rainwater into the gym.

He listened again for the muffled noise. What was it? Kaylee rummaging through the cleaning closet for the mop?

He paused again. Nothing seemed out of the ordinary, really, except for that one flicker of the security lights, something expected in a storm.

And the fact that Kaylee wasn't the kind to be disorganized. A police officer friend once jokingly called a neat desk the sign of a sick mind. A workplace should be disheveled and well lived in.

Kaylee's cleaning closet wouldn't be disorganized. She'd only be gone a moment. And that moment had passed minutes ago.

The cry reached him again and he straightened, listening more closely, through the rain and gale in his ears. And yet, above and beyond the elements, the hairs on the back of his head stood up.

The rain eased right then, from steady downpour to drizzle. Even over it, he found it hard to hear. And somewhere down the street, a road crew started a diesel truck.

Goose bumps rose on his skin.

He stepped gingerly over the river he'd made, then, with a sense of urgency growing exponentially, he found himself racing toward the side door.

When he reached the gym, he threw a fast glance one way up then the other. "Kaylee?"

He raced into the hall. Four doors, three of which stood closed. The last one was partially open.

He galloped down there. "Kaylee!"

With the light from the hall, he could see her on the floor.

His heart leapt in his throat. "Kaylee!" He dropped to her side.

Help me, Lord. Help us both.

She looked so pale, so small, so—

No! He pressed two fingers along the soft flesh of her throat.

A pulse. A pulse! She was alive! He glanced around. Nothing looked out of the ordinary to him… except that the dryer seemed pulled out. His gaze swept up past the machine, to settle on the mop handle behind it.

Had Kaylee pulled out the dryer to reach it? Had she slipped and fallen while pulling it back?

Hastily, he scanned the scene. In the next second, he lifted Kaylee's hand, ignoring her mild response of tugging back. Two red spots discolored the tips of her fingers, as if she'd been burned. From the dryer? He gasped, remembering that a few minutes ago, the security light outside had flickered. Had the dryer shocked her? Has she been lying here that long?

With tight lips and clenched jaw, he pulled her away from the dryer, did a quick primary survey according to his first-aid training, then, for the second time in a week, he scooped her up. And she was still far too light, far too delicate.

Lord, be with her.

In his arms, she shifted. He could feel her breath on his face as she stirred in his arms. Keeping himself steady with a wide stance, he rose.

He carried her down to the office, kicking the door open. The door slammed against a chair behind it and flung back to hit Eli's elbow as he barreled in.

Kaylee still lay limp in his arms. As he set her down on her side, her eyes opened and she groaned.

He threw back his head and laughed. Caught by his movement, a piece of paper from the nearby desk fluttered down on her. He set it back on the desk and laughed once more.

The clouds opened again and hard pellets of rain dashed against the window across the office from him. The overhead lights flickered once, twice, before steadying.

Kaylee flopped over onto her back, opened her mouth and blinked at him through the few hairs that had fallen in her face. "Why are you laughing?" she whispered hoarsely.

He sobered and drew her into his arms. "I'm just glad you're alive."

"Well, I sure don't feel that way." She groaned and with a grimace, rolled her shoulders.

Her beautiful face. His heart leaped into his throat. Her beautiful face scrunched up into a painful grimace.

"What happened?" she asked.

He tried to focus on her scraping words, but with the drumming rain and his own heart pounding in his throat, he couldn't manage. Finally, her words sank in.

"You don't remember?"

She shook her head and touched it gingerly. "No."

"I found you on the floor in front of the dryer."

She sat up, with one hand gripping Eli's and the other reaching for the top of the desk. That sheet of paper fluttered around with her movement, and she grabbed it and slammed it up on the desk. She winced and checked her fingers. "The dryer? I remember! I was electrocuted!"

"Shocked, actually. Electrocuted means you died by electricity."

"Whatever." She glanced down at her hand. "I slipped and grabbed the dryer. It gave me a shock. Whoa! I hit my head and my knee."

"A buffet of injuries for your first aider, hmm?" He reassessed her vitals, touching her forehead with the back of his hand and rechecking her pulse and breathing.

He stood, pulling her up with him, then setting her down in one of the chairs. After that, he called 9-1-1. Over the insistent drum of heavy rain, he gave a swift rundown of what had happened. Seeing the insistent shake of her head and the pleading in her eyes, he declined the ambulance for her.

Her color was much better, thankfully. Alert now, she listened to his report to the authorities.

"Why did you call 9-1-1?" she asked when he hung up. "I'm fine."

"You had a severe shock."

Kaylee leaned over and rubbed her knee. She then tested the feeling in her fingertips, all that with another pained expression.

She caught his stare. "I'm fine. And on a night like this one, we should save the ambulances for real emergencies. Besides, I can't afford one."

"I believe there's no charge in New Brunswick."

"Maybe so, but I don't want to owe you anything, thank you."

"Why?"

"Because—" She shut her mouth, but he knew the reason. He was Noah's brother. The sooner she was rid of him, the better.

With a bitter taste at the back of his mouth, he let the subject drop. His being there was bad enough for her.

A noise sounded at the far end. "Hello, anyone here?"

He jumped up and walked out into the hall. Officer Reading, the man he'd met in the vacant parking lot near the cul-de-sac, stood by the door.

"The dispatcher called us. We can't let a 9-1-1 call go unanswered. What's going on?"

Eli gave him the same rundown he'd given the dispatcher. He was actually glad that Reading had shown up. As a local in a position of authority, Reading might be able to convince Kaylee to see a doctor. Eli would take her, but he didn't think the hard feelings that might ensue would do their relationship any good.

Relationship? Did he and Kaylee actually have one?

"I don't need an ambulance," she was saying, "regardless of what Eli thinks. I got a nasty jolt, yes, but I feel fine. You can tell your dispatcher that, please."

Reading studied her, then nodded.

"I don't understand," Kaylee told the man after he'd finished speaking into his shoulder mike to cancel the ambulance. "I know the dryer is old, but I've touched it a hundred times or more. I've never been shocked by it."

Reading disappeared down the hall, only to return less than a minute later.

"Was it always pulled out like that? It seems as if it's sitting out about a foot more than it should be."

Kaylee frowned. "Yes, it is. I had to lean over to reach for the mop."

"What else is kept there besides the squeegee?" Reading asked.

"Not too much, just some stuff needed to tidy up the gym. A bit of vinegar for glass cleaner is the closest thing to chemicals we have here. Jenn is very sensitive to cleaning chemicals, so she insists that we only use natural products. I end up using a bit more elbow grease than I would expect. And a lot of old towels—"

She stopped speaking. Eli leaned forward. "What is it?"

"I actually slipped on the cement, thanks to these old boots and the puddle I made." She drew in a shivery kind of breath. "I guess they saved my life."

Eli exchanged a look with Reading. The officer spoke. "The rubber boots insulated you. And losing your balance helped you, too. You slipped away from the dryer."

Eli wanted to remind her who had orchestrated the events, but kept quiet. In Kaylee's mind, the Lord shouldn't have allowed it all to happen in the first place.

She stood and walked, however stiffly, into the hall, rubbing her neck as she went. Eli and the policeman followed. At the cleaning-room door, she stared in. "Perhaps Jenn pulled out the dryer. She's hopeful the town will buy a new one soon. This one's old and sometimes it didn't heat up."

Reading stepped past her.

"Don't touch anything," she cautioned him. "That dryer is live."

"I'll be careful." He had been bent down to peer at the dryer. Then, he strategically dropped a thin knifelike tool he'd pulled from his belt. The thing hit the floor at the same time a bright blue arc crossed from the dryer to the tip. Behind them the lights flickered. After the knife conducted the electricity, it clattered away from the dryer. With the tip of his boot, Reading pulled it closer to him and picked it up. "I'd say that dryer is quite live. Two hundred and twenty volts, with amperage to kill, I'm sure. Where's the circuit breakers? We should turn it off."

Kaylee told him where to find them. After several minutes and a few flickering lights, the dryer went dead.

Reading returned. "I'd say we've got cause for a new rec-center dryer now. That thing's shot." With a gingerly touch, he bounced his fingers off the top of the machine to test it. No sparks. Then, with his flashlight, he leaned over it to peer down the back.

"What do you see?" Kaylee asked.

"The rubber mat the dryer sits on is curled up here. And a few loose wires. It needs to be cleaned back here. Dust bunnies."

"Gee, thanks," she muttered.

"No offense was intended. Back of my dryer at home must be worse. Except I may not have as many candy wrappers in back of mine." He stooped down to pick one up.

Candy. Eli felt the color drain from his face, but kept his expression passive and his thoughts to himself. One member of Kaylee's church met Noah downtown here, walking distance from the store next to the center. The one that sold every piece of popular candy going. Noah had always loved candy.

"Can I take a look?" he asked the officer. Nodding, the man backed away from the dryer.

Eli took the flashlight Reading offered and peered in. He carefully surveyed the entire back of the dryer and the floor behind it. Leaning down, he wiggled the wires. They were loose and one even fell out onto the others from where it was set touching the outer case of the machine.

"We should ask Jenn if she moved this thing, and how far she went in disconnecting it," Reading said.

Eli looked up at him. "Why would she strip the wires and loosen them enough to touch each other? Why not just unplug it?"

"Those are questions for Jenn."

"I don't think she'd do it," Kaylee said. "She's too busy to waste time fooling around in here. Would she even know what to do?"

Reading looked at her. "Her father was the town

mechanic for years. Before she started to work here, she used to help him in his garage. She'd know what she was doing back there."

"She wouldn't loosen wires and leave them in such a hazardous way and then leave the circuit breaker on," Eli countered. "That would be plain stupid."

"Let's not jump to conclusions here." Reading answered. "Everyone makes mistakes. This is a minor accident. They're nearly all caused by stupidity."

"Jenn's not stupid," Kaylee argued. "I can't even see her doing this by accident."

"Maybe so. The only option right now is that someone doesn't like Jenn," Reading countered. "We all know she can be strict when it comes to the rules here. Even my own kids have complained about her telling them off."

Kaylee shot him an exasperated look. "Your son was kicking the volleyballs around. That's a big no-no and he knows it."

"He got grounded for that incident." He shrugged. "My point is that if there was foul play here, I'd suspect one of the teenagers first. My son said that they've started a new shop program at school about electricity. The kids may be experimenting. Has she caught the kids doing anything else wrong?"

Both Reading and Eli looked at Kaylee. She nodded. "Well, there were obscenities on the chalkboard of the women's change room, but we don't know who wrote them. You know the rules. Swearing isn't allowed. There's an automatic one-week suspension from the center."

Reading lifted his eyebrows. "Then if this was deliberate, whoever did this was after Jenn and we were just plain fortunate that you didn't get hurt too badly." He peered at her. "You really should get checked out by a doctor."

Kaylee lowered her gaze. Frustration rose in Eli. "He's right, you know? If you won't let us call an ambulance, I'll take you in myself. Kaylee, you've been shocked and hit your head. You have to be seen by a doctor!"

She touched her head and winced. If she'd allow him to check her, he knew he'd find a goose egg there. And she'd say she couldn't afford to take time off—not while the remnants of a hurricane flooded the gym.

Reading flicked off his flashlight, just as his radio crackled. He spoke on it briefly before looking at her again. "I've got to go. The road by the park is flooding. If you think of anything else that I should know, I'm going to be around all night. And," he added, focusing his attention on Eli, "if there's anything you think we can do to help, let me know, okay?"

With a nod, he left.

Eli heard Kaylee sigh. He could guess her thoughts. They were as easy to read as the defeated look on her face.

"I better call Jenn," she said, walking back into the office. She looked tired, pale and ready to drop

"Sit," Eli ordered. "I'll call her. She'll want to come in."

Kaylee had seen enough doctors since she escaped from the compound. The doctor that the police ordered and then several in the last two weeks alone. They all meant well, all gave her sound advice, but she was sick of being poked and prodded and questioned.

But she was secretly glad Eli was now driving her into the city. She wouldn't waste an ambulance and didn't see that she needed one. But now, over an hour after Eli had found her, nearly to the hospital in Fredericton, she found herself wilting exceptionally fast.

Following her directions, Eli sped up toward the emergency room's entrance. An ambulance was just pulling out, its lights still winking. The streets all over the city were drenched and deserted, but the hospital was buzzing.

Eli got her in and registered. The clerk informed them that parts of the city were without power and several nursing homes were being evacuated—some of the residents were ending up at the hospital.

"We'll try to get you in as soon as possible," she told Kaylee with a sympathetic smile.

True to her word, the clerk called out her name a few minutes later. Eli went in with Kaylee, a fact that she was glad for. The doctor examined her. Her head wound was nothing serious, though she was given a list of things to watch out for. Then he checked all her vitals, saying in the end that it was the rubber boots that kept her from being a better conductor. Although only a few milliamperes could kill, she appeared to have a higher resistance than most.

"Perhaps it's your lack of body fat. You are one lucky woman," he said as he finished his exam.

"Luck had nothing to do with it," Eli stated after the doctor left.

She let him help her off the exam table. "Eli, how

can I be grateful that God saved my life, when He could have prevented the accident in the first place?"

He said nothing, but held her hand. Then, a moment later, he pulled her into a tight embrace. Talking into her hair, he said, "There are a hundred answers to that question, Kaylee. And every one of them valid and worth saying. But would you believe them?"

"Maybe."

"If you were told by someone that you'd get hurt if you went to work today, would you listen to that person and not go to work?"

She lifted her head from his shoulder, meeting his still, soft blue eyes. "It depends on who it was."

"Only a very trusted friend would be able to convince you to stay home, right?"

"Yes."

"Is there anyone in Riverline that you can call a really close, trusted friend?"

She stared down at his jacket, thinking. "Lois cares for me, but she has her family. I have friends back home. Good, trustworthy friends. But, no, no one living in Riverline I would call a really trusted friend."

She dared a look into his face, to somehow measure his sincerity. He wasn't smiling. In fact, in the examination room, where the lights were coldly fluorescent, his features looked pale and drawn. The expression was of worry.

Eli was fast becoming the only trusted friend she had here, a thought that tightened her chest and yet didn't sit well. "The job was the only thing that brought me here," she said. "My counselor found the house I rent and the job, too. I just took it all."

"So you haven't seen your friends back home yet?"

"I called a couple when I first moved to Riverline. I promised I'd go down for a visit soon."

She felt his grip tighten. "But you haven't. Why?"

She tried to lift her shoulders to shrug her answer, but he held her tight.

"So you may not even listen to a trusted friend if they warn you, right?"

She lifted her shoulders. "I'd listen. I would respect them that much." She paused. "But…I would probably go to work. I need the money and it would have to make very clear sense to me not to go."

Eli pulled her back into his arms and held her there, snugly. His words didn't make sense. For instance, why did he avoid the issue of God? Why didn't he use this moment to evangelize? Surprise settled into her as she realized that maybe she was ready to hear Eli's thoughts on God.

But there were no words for her. Instead, Eli held her close and she could feel his rapid heartbeat, his shallow breathing and what she could only describe as his shaking body.

Then she felt his lips on her hair, warm, touching, almost loving. A gentle gift that left her heart pounding as fast as his was.

"You look a mess," Jenn announced as Kaylee and Eli returned to the center. All three stood at the entrance to the gym, but with the mop in hand, Jenn was in the middle of a battle with the water that had spread across the gym floor.

Thankfully, she looked as if she was winning. She smiled at Kaylee. "But I'm glad they didn't keep you overnight."

Kaylee turned away. "I'll get another mop," she said, also thankful.

"Whoa!" Jenn answered her. Kaylee turned. Both Eli and her boss were standing there. While Jenn just gaped at her, Eli scowled.

"You're in no shape to do any work," he said.

"I can't just leave Jenn with this mess!"

"It's half done, now, and I can help her."

Kaylee stepped forward. "I wasn't hurt that bad," she argued back. "I bumped my head and the shock I got barely hurt." She wiggled her fingers. "See? Everything's normal."

Eli's scowl deepened. "I disagree. Especially since we don't know how the accident happened in the first place. It could have easily been a deliberate act and whether against you or Jenn, it doesn't matter. You were hurt and you're better off going home."

"It was just an accident," she insisted.

Jenn stepped between them, still tucking the mop under her arm as she lifted both hands. She looked at Eli then at Kaylee. "No, it wasn't an accident."

TWELVE

Eli and Kaylee cut short their argument to stare at Jenn.

She led them into the hall, stopping at the cleaning room. "I did it."

"How?" Kaylee asked. "Why?"

Jenn laughed self-consciously. "It wasn't to kill you, if that's what you're thinking. I pulled the dryer out in order to clean behind it. I didn't want you doing it because you're still not strong enough."

Kaylee opened her mouth to protest, but Jenn held up her hand. "And I knew if I told you what I was doing, you'd get defensive." She turned to Eli. "The town has agreed to buy the center another washer and dryer. This pair is on its last legs. I'm even allowed to pick the set out. I've ordered them from the catalogue and they were supposed to be delivered tomorrow."

"So why did you loosen the wires at the back instead of unplugging it?"

"I didn't. I meant to unplug it, but the phone rang and I left it. Then I forgot." She faced Kaylee again, looking stricken. "I'm so sorry! I didn't realize the wires were loose and the machine posed a hazard. I'd have never left it like that. I feel awful."

Kaylee automatically reached out to rub her boss's arm. "It's okay. But the wires, how did they get so loose? Eli says the ground is off and another live wire was touching the outside."

"That dryer has been vibrating all over the room for years. It's as though something inside is out of balance. It's worse than the washer, believe me. I came in one morning last year and found it jammed up against the door. I could hardly get into the room. It's as if the thing has a mind of its own."

Though she didn't feel like smiling, Kaylee did so anyway. "But I don't remember you telling me about getting a new washer and dryer."

Jenn offered a sheepish look. "That's my fault again. I didn't tell you, but I did put the memo from the council in your box. You didn't see it?"

She shook her head. "The only thing in my box was my check."

Jenn frowned. "I should have photocopied it. Drat. I need that memo, too, for my files. One councillor wants to rescind the offer, saying he didn't sign it and I know his initials were on the paper. I wonder where it is." She strode out of the room and down into the office, Kaylee and Eli following her.

After a hasty search, she found it. The desk beside where she'd awoken after getting shocked, Kaylee noted. She'd grabbed that very same memo and shoved it on the desk after it had fluttered down on her head. But the desk wasn't assigned to anyone.

Eli lifted his brows. "I put that up there. It fell off when I laid Kaylee down."

"Hmm," Jenn murmured. "I was sure I put it in your box. Oh, well, we have it now and you aren't too badly hurt. But you're not working tonight. Your man here can take you home."

Kaylee opened her mouth to protest the term Jenn used, but after spying Jenn's smug smile, decided not to invite more mischief. She shut her mouth. Eli wasn't her man. And he wasn't looking for a permanent home here in Riverline or anywhere in Canada for that matter. So making him *her man* was just looking for heartache.

"Let's go," Eli said, taking her arm. Despite her internal rebuke, his touch felt good and she found herself leaning in close to him. "I can come back and help Jenn."

"Thanks." Was she really heading for another big sorrow in her life? Just him touching her arm sent shivers of excitement through her. She liked Eli's gentle touch.

Whoa. This whole situation was getting out of hand, Kaylee decided as she thanked Jenn with a small smile. She'd lost both parents and her beloved sister. Now she was looking at another painful heartache if she thought that anything could come out of this curious relationship she'd developed with Eli.

Besides, hadn't he, in the backyard, warned her all men were alike? She'd be crazy not to heed his words.

She had to do something, force him to leave before she got hurt. So what could she do?

There was one way. She could go home. Leave Riverline.

The rain eased over the next twelve hours. And despite the flooded basements and washed-out roads around the area, the late morning air held a cleansed feel. Kaylee had already been out for her walk. She was gaining more endurance, more strength. Her mind slipped back to last night when Eli refused to allow her to work.

She should have helped.

Having seen her return, Lois had already called her to ask if her basement was still dry, adding that the River Road had crumbled in one spot.

Kaylee was due to go back to work that afternoon, and as she set down the phone, she found she was asking herself one question.

Would Eli come with her? He'd spent a week in Riverline and, despite all the difficult issues and the terrible accident, too, she'd enjoyed his company. Last night, he'd been a thankful addition to the cleanup crew, but it wouldn't be long before he'd hear from his investigator about Phoebe. Then he'd be gone. If she didn't give him a reason to leave before that. Like leaving first.

Her heart squeezed. She quickly shut the front door and locked it, preparing to walk to work.

Yet as she trotted down her narrow driveway, another question lingered. Was Eli hanging around to find Noah? She'd heard through the center's grapevine that Hec Haines had claimed to have met Eli and yet she'd heard that Eli denied it.

There was only one answer to Hec's mistake.

Noah was in Riverline.

Why hadn't Eli mentioned that to her? Was he trying to protect her? Or was the rumor just that, a rumor?

To counter her crazy heartbeat, she straightened her shoulders. *You'll keep me safe, won't You, Lord? Please?*

She picked up the pace, wondering briefly if she was running away from her prayer or from Noah. Or from the feelings for Eli growing within her?

Running where, though? Like Lois, her aunt had called that morning, anxious to hear how she'd weathered the storm. She also wanted to know if she was coming down before Christmas, or even during the holidays, for that matter. Kaylee had heard the sadness in her voice, the concern, too, and it had cut into her.

"Kaylee!"

She looked up. Coming down the cul-de-sac was Eli. She stopped and watched him. A week ago she'd fainted, thinking he was Noah. But now, seeing Eli every day, she could see the differences in the two men. Eli's walk was straighter, his movements more fluid, his frame stronger. Yes, he was more tanned, like she had suspected that evening on her back deck when the setting sun tricked her.

When she turned, she noticed his face light up. Seeing his reaction, she felt her breath catch in her throat.

And found herself smiling at him. "Hi. Not too tired this afternoon?"

He glanced at his watch. "Not quite noon yet. And, no, I'm not tired." He rolled his left shoulder. "Though I'm a bit sore from mopping most of the night."

"I'm really grateful that you stayed and helped. You didn't have to."

"I was glad to. I just hope no more came in after we left."

"I don't expect so. Lois says the town workers have been out all night, so I expect that they sandbagged everything and checked out the back of the gym."

"I hope I didn't embarrass myself with my sandbagging skills. I may be a bit rusty."

"When did you do it last?"

He grinned. "Never."

She chuckled. "I'm sure it was fine."

His smile dissolved away. "Someone had moved those sandbags from where you said they were. Recently, I'd say, by the stain left. It caused the water from the downspout to drain straight under the gym door."

"Did you tell Jenn?"

"No. I didn't want the kids to get into any more trouble than they were already."

"Like Officer Reading's boy?"

"From what you say, he can get into enough trouble without any help from me."

"True." She wanted to ask him about his conversation with Hec Haines. But the right words wouldn't form in her mouth. Should she be repeating rumors? Accusing him of keeping things from her? Did she even want to know his answer?

No.

They fell into step along the sidewalk. For several minutes, they walked in a comfortable silence. Funny how he'd come into her routine and settled in so easily.

"Have you heard from your investigator?" Even as she spoke those words, she regretted them. He was ready to leave town on his quest at any moment.

Why had she asked such an obvious and painful question in the first place?

Eli didn't want to talk about his investigator. Not with Kaylee. And not now.

"Did you go for a walk this morning?"

She nodded and kept up her brisk pace.

"Was that wise? You were hurt quite badly last night."

"The fresh air helped my headache. Besides, I've got that list of things to look out for. It didn't say to take it easy."

"But that would be for a person of normal good health."

"You sound like my aunt. She called this morning to see how I weathered the storm."

"Did you tell her about last night?"

"No. I didn't want to worry her." She slowed her walk, adding, "She asked me when I was coming home for a visit. Two weeks ago, I was so sure I didn't want to deal with my hometown and rehash everything that has happened to each person I speak to, but now I don't know. I can't bring back Trisha. I want to put all of this behind me. Start afresh. And if that means clearing the air in my hometown, so be it."

He digested her quiet, anxious words. She should go home. She wanted to. Her aunt, her only living relative as far as he knew, should see her. Her friends, too, could help her.

Where would that leave him?

Selfishly wanting her to stay, that's where. Phoebe had been bang on with her accusation.

And what would Noah do? Discover that there were more people who meant something to Kaylee, more people to torment and hurt with his revenge?

He grit his teeth. *I'm not being selfish, Phoebe.*

At the end of her street, they turned left. Ahead,

numerous orange pylons indicated where the road had become unstable and, several meters beyond that, a sign pointed to a detour. Curious townspeople had come out to inspect the road for themselves.

"River Road is impassible," he said, glad for the change of his focus. "I had to cut through the park down by the river. It was nearly underwater, too."

They picked their way around the pylons toward the park. The wind had stripped the trees. Now the bright red maple leaves lay slick and matted in bold splotches along the road.

At the end, they saw the damage in the full light of day. A huge gouge of chewed up asphalt served now as the lining for a pool of rainwater. Several workers were busying pumping it dry. Along the other way, leaves smothered the storm drains and the water was backing up along the curbs.

"This way," Eli said, guiding Kaylee around the hole toward the park. The storm had flattened what annuals had survived the frost of a few nights ago. They had to step onto the wet grass in several spots to avoid large puddles. Eli automatically glanced at Kaylee's feet. Like most others out, she wore rain boots, the same secondhand cracked gum rubbers she'd worn the night before.

All he had were his hiking boots and he could feel the dampness seeping in between his toes.

Toward the end, the park rose slightly and widened. They could see that most of the small trees and shrubs had fared better here. And thankfully, so did the short pedestrian bridge over the creek.

Eli could hear the rushing water as they rounded the path toward the bridge. With his gaze, he followed the

swollen creek's meandering line to where it cut under River Road. After that, it wandered off to the far side of the playground and the rec center.

Still, the town workers were using its close proximity as a drain. Behind them, the steady drone of Wajax pumps filled the air.

Kaylee stepped on the leaf-strewn bridge, slowing down to peer over the railing. Eli stood back a moment.

"Lois said this creek normally dries up by fall. Look at it now."

Eli watched her instead. To anyone else, he imagined she looked fine, without any great concerns in her life. But there were concerns and the biggest was his brother. He could see the carefully disguised pain in her eyes.

Was Noah responsible for what happened last night?

As Eli started toward her, his cell phone whirred. Reaching into his jacket pocket for it, he paused a few meters from the edge of the bridge. "Hello?"

"Eli, it's me."

Roger, his investigator. Eli's heart hammered as he glanced up to see Kaylee shift to other side of the bridge. The dark, thick shrubs behind her framed her slim form. "What did you find out?"

"Good news." Roger said. "Several women matching the descriptions you gave me were seen southeast of Tallahassee, Florida. At a campground."

He perked up. "Are you sure? Were there any men with them?"

"I hired a couple who've helped me out before to check on them. But so far, no sign of any men."

"They usually don't travel without a man in the group. No one who fits Noah's description?"

"No men period. Just a couple of children. From what I've learned, one of the women fits Phoebe's description."

Eli's heart drummed in his ears, drowning out the distant sound of the pumps and the rush of water ahead. He could hardly breathe. This was good news. Great news! Locating The Farm in Maine had been a blessing for sure, but he hadn't been able to confirm Phoebe was still with them, not until meeting Kaylee.

Now he had a woman fitting her description. It had to be her!

"Can you fly down?" Roger asked.

A blur of movement in his peripheral vision and he looked up.

Kaylee was gone. A thin line had been drawn through the wet carpet of fallen leaves, from the center of the bridge to the far side.

"Eli, you there?"

He ignored his investigator. "Kaylee?"

No answer. Eli shoved his phone into his pocket. He hurried onto the bridge in time to see the bright blue of her jacket sweep under the rushing water below.

A hand reached out, wildly grasping for the rocks that lined the high sides of the creek.

Kaylee!

He let out a strangled noise, tore off his jacket and bolted over the railing to plunge into the soft, sodden edge of the bank.

Kaylee's head cleared the water and their gazes locked. Then she went under again.

He slid down the bank toward the mouth of the creek, digging into the mess of tangled growth and eroding soil until his foot caught an outcropped rock.

Kaylee was already sweeping past him as he thrust out his hand. He caught her wrist when she reached out again. With a sudden strength, he hauled hard. Her head broke the water, then her shoulders. He half twisted around and grabbed a weakened alder with his free hand. And hung on.

His foot slipped into the rushing water, but found a shelf of flat stone, securing his grip.

"Eli!"

Kaylee's cry sliced through him, spurring him to tug harder. She grazed over the lower bank until she could find her own footing on the rocks. Her free hand flailed out to grab the small bushes that grew along the vertical bank.

"Hang on!" He secured his footing again, found another alder to grab and pulled again. Kaylee was halfway up the bank by that time.

A moment later, they both lay on the top, not far from bridge, partially hidden in the wild growth of shrubbery that still wore brilliant red leaves.

Eli dropped his head onto the ground and sighed. "Are you all right?"

Beside him, Kaylee coughed.

He sat up, wincing at the aches forming from his slide down the bank. "What happened?"

Shivering, she shoved the hair from her eyes and blinked at him. "I just slipped. The wood planks seemed to be covered in an oily film. Add those leaves and boy, it's slippery!" She shook her head. "It hap-

pened so fast. First I was watching the water, then I was sliding right under the railing."

She leaned forward, scanning the bridge. "I walked over that bridge this morning and it wasn't like that. I even stopped and talked to someone. Neither of us slipped then and there weren't any leaves, either."

Eli glanced around the park. As nice as it was, there were none of the bold sugar maples whose leaves now lined the bridge. The closest were upriver and downwind.

He rose to inspect the bridge, skimming his fingertips over the boards, then rubbing them together. "Who did you talk to?" he asked.

"Just one of the shopkeepers, I think. I told her about the gym and that I was planning to come back this afternoon. She'd spent the night at her shop herself." She leaned forward to pull off her boot and rub her ankle, pulling back the sodden sock to peer at the skin. He heard her gasp.

"What's wrong?"

"I don't know. Look at this cut. I don't remember slicing it on anything. I must have hit something sharp. It sliced right through my rubber boot."

Eli shifted to take her foot in his hands. A thin welt had already formed across her ankle. The center of the cut had begun to ooze blood.

He shifted over to the edge of the bridge, feeling the wet ground until he found what he suspected had cut her.

The same type of wire Noah had used for tripping his homemade bombs.

The Wajax pumps down the street stopped abruptly. A truck that had been backing up near them had its engine suddenly cut.

Static reached past the sound of fast flowing water. Then a weak voice called out. "Eli, are you there?"

His jacket lay where he'd tossed it, and his cell phone, still connected to his investigator, remained shoved in the pocket. But the voice still reached him.

Kaylee tugged on her sock. "Who is that you were talking to?"

He swallowed. "My investigator. He found Phoebe."

"Oh." She looked away.

Eli met her shy concern by lifting her jaw up with his finger. "But I can't leave."

"You aren't going? Why?"

A dark cloud drifted in front of the sun, dimming the park and cooling the already brisk wind. Eli stood, helped her up and then brought his jacket over. He took his cell phone out before draping the jacket over her shoulders. The open connection crackled again. Eli lifted it to his ear. "Can I call you back?" Without another word, he disconnected.

"We should get you inside." He glanced around. A group of teenagers were making their way down the path toward them.

With his hands, he swept the fallen leaves off the bridge. He quickly grabbed several handfuls of dirt from underneath the shrubs and spread them out on the slippery section of wood. Brushing off his hands, he said, "Let's go to the gym. Do you have a change of clothes there?"

Kaylee nodded. Together, they hurried across the street.

"Let's go in on this side." She pointed to the right. "My locker's closest to that door and I think there's been enough water brought into the gym lately."

Inside and waiting for Kaylee to change, Eli called his investigator back. "Sorry about that. We had an accident."

"Anyone hurt?"

"No."

"So, when can you get here?"

Eli tightened his lips to a thin line. He could hear the plop of wet clothes inside the women's change room, before the sound of the electric hand dryer drowned it all out.

Lord, what should I do? All these years and You've finally given me Phoebe. And shown me Kaylee—

"Eli?"

"I don't know when I can get down there."

Roger made a soft disapproving noise. "I'm not sure how long these women are going to stay put. They're only camping and don't seem to have enough supplies."

Frustration welled in him. He needed time. He needed to think. To pray. And Kaylee was finished changing.

She threw open the change-room door, dressed in a pair of well-worn green sweatpants and a soft, matching sweatshirt that bore the town logo. She'd only half dried her hair, then tossed it back. Though wet, it shone softly in a sweet, messy way.

He swallowed. How could he leave her?

"Hey, what do you want me to do?"

Eli stared down at his phone. He couldn't afford his investigator much longer. And the man had other clients. He lifted the phone back to his ear. "Can you get a shot of Phoebe and e-mail it to me? I want to be sure it's her."

"Sure. I'll ask that couple to get one."

As he shut his cell phone, Eli knew what was happening.

Kaylee was beginning to mean something to him and he couldn't leave her, not with his brother lurking about. Her church's congregation may care for her, one of them may even be an auxiliary police officer, but they didn't know Noah the way he did.

And Noah wasn't going to take Kaylee like he took Phoebe.

THIRTEEN

Kaylee worked all afternoon, tidying up the office and the change rooms, refusing to dwell on all that had happened to her. When she got to the cleaning room, both she and Jenn chatted as they swept and prepared for the new appliances.

One thing she didn't mention was the accumulation of candy wrappers on the floor behind the dryer. Being a health nut, Jenn would never eat candy and she remembered Eli's concern about getting the kids into more trouble. Best to just sweep them up and forget about them.

With Jenn not one to dawdle, they got the room gleaming in no time. Shortly after that, Eli returned to drive her home. Where he'd gone, she didn't ask, telling herself it was none of her business. But had it something to do with the call he'd made while she was changing?

About Phoebe? Her heart clenched at the thought of him leaving and she hated the selfishness within her.

As they pulled into her driveway, Kaylee glanced at Lois's home. Would the older lady be keeping an eye out for her? Kaylee didn't date. She didn't do anything in the evenings she didn't work. Which meant if she wasn't home, Lois could be concerned.

But if Lois saw her now, she'd be shocked. Despite changing, Kaylee still had that bedraggled look. It came partly from the change of clothes, partly from shock, partly from too much work.

Partially from the realization that Eli would be leaving soon.

She threw open the car door. Beside her, Eli sat quietly. They'd said no more about his decision to remain in Riverline because Jenn had chosen that moment to walk into the rec center. A thousand unasked questions still burned through her.

"Kaylee?"

She turned. In the dim glow from the streetlights, now on so early, Eli's face appeared less harsh. His solemn profile tugged at her heart. Still gripping the steering wheel, he leaned toward her and swallowed. "I'm sorry for all that's happened."

Tears pricked in her eyes. He meant it. She could see the empathy in his eyes, hear the shake in his voice. "I know. And I'm sorry that..."

No, she wouldn't tell him she was sorry he wasn't leaving to find Phoebe. Besides the fact it was rude, it simply wasn't true.

She climbed out, feeling the aches of all that had happened in her legs and arms. She'd no sooner shut the passenger door, than Eli climbed out. "Wait!" He strode around the front of his car. For the briefest of moments, she felt as though this was the end of a date.

It wasn't. Nor would she pretend it was. "Kaylee. This isn't over for you."

She stopped. "What do you mean?"

"You know what I mean. Noah isn't finished. He's here, toying with you."

The truth she'd been skirting all week rocked her now. With a bite on her lips, she stepped back. "No. He's gone. The police said he's moved south. No one would bomb their own home if they planned to return."

"He has no intention of returning there. He rigged his compound to explode because he knew I'd come looking for Phoebe. Like scuttling a ship. And he may have even watched it explode. Regardless, he's here. I know him. I can feel it. My investigator said only the women are in Florida. Do you know how that could be?"

"No. The women never went anywhere without the men, but we didn't have that many men. Noah, John, Wilf, who married Tina, and another man, Thomas. But I get the impression that Thomas isn't the faithful sort. As for Wilf, he and Tina started having problems after their child died."

Eli frowned, leaving her to regret she'd brought up that terrible incident. Thankfully, he didn't ask for more details.

But he did speak. "So it's possible that there aren't any men with them?"

Her throat dried and tightened. She shook her head, feeling confused. "Noah *is* insane, but he's not after me. Your investigator is mistaken. Those women would never go south alone."

"I know my brother. I know what he's capable of. And what he'll do. He'll come after you, Kaylee. He warned you that he would."

"He warned me that he'd kill Trisha if I left. So that means *I* killed her by leaving."

"No, you didn't! Noah did. Don't let him poison your mind. I know he told you if anything happened to her, you'd be at fault, but you're not." He grabbed her shoulders. "And you're not safe here, either. Remember, he threatened you!"

She stepped back from him, closing in on her home. "Don't say that!"

"And you know Lois's dog? He's dead. He was the dog that was killed that night. The one that stopped barking right after a painful yelp. Did you ask Lois what was wrong with him?"

"I've been too busy and Lois didn't mention anything." She searched his face. "What happened?"

Eli's face showed reluctance. "Suffice it to say that his barking was a problem to Noah. And it was Noah."

She leaned away, trying not to absorb all he was saying. That poor dog! "Crazy or not, Noah's done with me. Haven't I been through enough this past year? You should know that more than anyone. Noah's gone, so if I were you, I'd be heading south while the trail's still fresh." She wrenched herself free and raced to her door.

Her heart pounded against her ribs as she struggled to unlock the deadbolt.

"Kaylee!"

"Just leave me alone!" She threw her comment over her shoulder.

Her fingers shook as she rushed inside. Once safely there, she found her breath heaving as she slid to the floor. She hated being so helpless, so useless, so stupidly fearful. She'd been like that for two years and she never wanted to be like that again. But here she was, weak, powerless, not even strong enough to want to fight back.

Eli found her minutes later. Wordlessly, he lifted her up and took her into her living room. She slumped down on the couch, her head hitting the back cushion.

He found her a pillow to hug, which she snatched and drew to her chest. Then he spoke. "Noah isn't done yet. You've got to believe me."

"I don't want to hear that. You're sounding like a broken record. Noah's gone. He fled south. He's taken them all, including Phoebe, with him. Don't waste time with me. You want Phoebe, so you shouldn't be hanging around here."

"I know my brother. And I know he's here."

"Don't say that! It's not—"

"It is true! Let me tell you how I know. Hec Haines talked to him last Thursday night. When I saw Hec at church, he began to talk to me as if he'd already met me. He had met Noah, who was impersonating me. What better way to stick around town than to pretend to be someone else? We look enough alike to fool most strangers and he knows I've been all over town." He pushed further. "And you already said that he warned he would kill you."

Her head shot up. "No, I didn't!"

"Yes, you did. When we first met, you said something about Noah threatening to kill you."

Feeling the blood drain from her face, she looked up at him. "I said that?"

"Don't you remember? Right outside here? You said he would kill you. Then at the compound, when you panicked?"

She frowned, deep in thought. After she swallowed, started to speak, stopped and started again. "I did. Oh, no!"

He reached out to help her, but she jumped up and away from him. "No! This isn't fair! I don't deserve it!"

She stalked away, only to stop, spin and return. "Forget it! This is *not* happening to me!"

He grabbed her. "It is! But I can help you."

She shrugged him off. "I've started over. I have friends here. They'll help me."

"But they can't protect you from Noah. They don't know him like I know him."

She scrunched up her eyes before throwing up her hands to cover her face. When he held out his arms to draw her close, she didn't resist.

They clung to each other for a long time, until, stiff and sore, she peeled free of him and sank down on the couch.

Peeking up at him, she watched him offer up a quiet prayer.

Lord in Heaven, help us both, she added when he'd finished. *Please.* Because she had the feeling Eli needed His help more now than he ever did before.

Five minutes later, she found Eli in the kitchen, making coffee.

He looked across the small room at her. When she didn't speak, he looked over at her questioningly.

"I…I need to talk to you." She dropped into the nearest chair, hoping the look on her face wasn't as blank as it felt. She had no idea what was in her heart, let alone what she could say.

Eli sat down beside her. After a short silence, he suggested softly, "Why don't we pray first?"

She stiffened. "It won't do any good. I don't mean to be disrespectful, but I've done all kinds of praying these past two years and nothing good ever happened. I prayed in the living room after you did and I don't feel any different." She struggled to find the best words. "I even prayed while I was in that compound and all that I got was more involved with them. I ended up believing the lies Noah told. The whole time I was praying for help, but I got nothing back, no peace, no hope, nothing!"

Eli smiled. "So, what you're saying is that you want me to pray instead of you?"

Despite the turmoil within her, Kaylee snickered. It was more of a nervous laugh, but it was nice to see a different side to Eli. Had his decision to stay lifted a weight from him? "Go ahead. You'd do better than me, anyway."

They bowed their heads. Taking her hands, he said a soft prayer.

It was lovely. Gentle, thankful words rich with a deep sense of commitment. Kaylee bit back the wash of longing she felt. To have that kind of faith; to know peace and trust was just a prayer away.

"So," he said after he'd finished, "you need to talk?"

"I…" She didn't know where to start. To her horror, she felt an unwelcome swell of tears and looked at Eli through watery eyes. "You say that Noah's here. How? What are we…"

She couldn't hold back the tears anymore. For a few minutes, she sobbed quietly. Honestly, would she ever be strong again?

Eli found a box of tissues and, after setting it down in front of her, he held her hand. When she finally pulled herself together, she blinked up at him. He was sitting there, his eyes closed.

Praying again?

Oh, how good it would feel to rely on God, to totally believe He'd help, that He cared for people like her.

Eli opened his eyes. Without speaking, he rose and walked into her living room. There, she watched as he scribbled something down on a sheet of cut-up scrap paper she always kept by the phone.

Fascinated by his smooth, fluid movements, she felt a warmth grow in her heart as he wrote swiftly.

With his left hand.

She stiffened. His left hand? Eli was left-handed. She knew that.

The warmth of a moment ago drained, replaced by a cold, icy clutch around her heart.

When he returned to the kitchen and sat down again, he looked at her. He went instantly alert. "Something's wrong. What's going on?"

Rubbing her arms, she chewed on her lip. "Noah has been here."

"I know. Hec Haines met him downtown."

"No, I mean, here, at this house. In the backyard. And I was ready to let him just walk in and be alone with me!"

FOURTEEN

Noah had been here? Right in Kaylee's backyard? Toying with her, just as Eli knew his brother would. He pushed himself to his feet, anger fueling his movements. "Are you sure about that?"

"Yes. I went out on the deck a couple of nights ago and he was down on the lawn. It was nearly dark, and I—I thought he was you and he let me believe that."

"What were you doing out there?"

"I saw the leash."

"Leash?"

"Pepe's leash. I saw it tangled around the deck railing and went out to see what it was. Then I saw someone standing underneath and…I said something. He stepped out from under the deck and started to talk to me. He let me think that he was you."

Eli dug his fingers through his short hair. Noah knew his younger brother was here, glancing over his shoulder at every opportunity, being everywhere as much as possible. Eli hadn't slept much since he came, choosing instead to learn every trail, every teenage hangout, every inch of this small town.

Only a matter of time before he found Noah. A

short time if he knew that Noah was coming around here.

In front of him, Kaylee was rubbing her arms. He wanted to warm her up, hold her tight and tell her that everything would be fine. But first he needed some information. "What else did he say? What did he do? Did you see which way he went?"

She shook her head. "No. It was as if he went poof and was gone, like in those scary movies when you turn around and the person has disappeared. How did he learn I was here?"

"Probably the same way I learned. I hired someone to find you." Eli stilled. Noah and he not only looked alike, they could easily be mistaken for each other on the phone. A man as crafty as Noah might find out who Eli had hired—

Or he could have done his own legwork, pretending to be Eli.

No time to waste with speculation. "Did he look wet, as if he'd been standing outside for a while? Did he look in any way cold?"

With a quick lick of her lips, she shook her head again. "It hadn't begun to rain yet. Well, if anything, he looked a bit too smug." She shivered. "I can't believe I was fooled. This is insane. Noah's insane!"

Her words sobered him and he frowned, absorbing the full impact of what she meant. "I know it wasn't me, but what made you realize it was him?"

"I didn't until just now. He used his right hand to untangle Pepe's leash. I didn't realize it at the time, but just now watching you write made me remember." As if charged with strong insight, she stood. "And I've been finding candy wrappers on the floor at the rec center. I thought it was the kids, but lately, most have been stuck on some new cartoon's candy—marshmallow stuff made into different faces. These wrappers belonged to the hard candies made in the store next to the gym."

He wasn't following her thoughts. "But what's these candies got to do with Noah?"

"I smelled them on him, along with some other yucky smell."

He lifted his eyebrows. "Yucky?"

"Bad is more like it. It smelled like rotten eggs. I only got a short whiff, but it was the sweet, minty scent that stood out. I remembered it because I smelled it at the center."

"Which is beside the candy store."

"Yes, which must..." As her voice died away, he stood, pivoting slowly as he straightened. All the while, he said nothing. His shoulders ached, his head was beginning to pound and he fought the urge to grab Kaylee and tell her to throw stuff into a suitcase. Despite his cool, calm actions, his thoughts were churning. Take her far away, at top speed, as if the world were on fire.

But did God want him to go? He shut his eyes. *What should I do, Lord? I want to do Your will.*

When he opened his eyes, he found Kaylee studying him. The urge to explain swelled. "I'm trying to figure out what to do."

"Were you praying?"

"Saying a short one, yes. But often, when God wants me to do something, I get a strong urge to do that. It's immediate and I often say yes without really thinking of what I'm saying." He offered a half smile. "It's hard to explain. I just get a good feeling that what I'm doing is the right thing to do."

"Are you getting that sense now? What do you think we should do? Call the police?"

He lifted his eyebrows. "Yes, I'll call Reading. He'll want to know this has happened. But as for what we should do, I don't know." He hated that he sounded so defeated. "I mean, not yet, anyway."

Her expression closed, turning critical. "Is it fair for us to have to wait at such a crucial time? Would God be so cruel to do that to us?"

"No, He wouldn't. But sometimes He lets us work on our own, even to the point of allowing us to make mistakes. I want to take you away from here, right now. But I don't know if that's the right thing to do."

"Lois has a Christian CD of a group that sings about whether it's God or Satan talking."

"Exactly. I don't know if I should take you somewhere safe or stay to find Noah."

"Take me somewhere? I'm not a child, Eli. Don't treat me like one."

He flicked up his eyebrows. "You're right, of course."

Her expression softened immediately. Her mouth parted as though she wanted to say something, but no words came. With her dark hair and that wide-eyed expression of half fear and half trust, she bore such heart-wrenching innocence. He shouldn't be talking about the evil one, and not knowing what to do. These thoughts were his personal ones, part of his own journey. They were too intimate for sharing.

Yet he wanted to share them with her. And with her so close, so needing the warm comfort of someone she trusted, he also wanted badly to take hold of her.

To kiss her, help her forget their danger.

She blinked and the beguiling expression vanished.

"What I don't understand is why Noah declined my invitation to come inside? I mean, I thought he was you and asked him in for coffee. He had the perfect opportunity to kill me, or at least destroy my faith in you."

She had faith in him? He felt the start of a smile at the comment. "What did he say? Just no?"

She shook her head. "Not quite. He said that men couldn't be trusted. That he was just like Noah. I mean, he was talking as though he were you, letting me think that, and said that he—you, I mean—were just like him." She rubbed her forehead, obviously struggling with the situation. "I kept disagreeing with him."

Before he could answer, she groaned and threw back her head. "He said that all men were alike and that he couldn't be trusted any more than anyone else. To be alone with a woman, that is. He sounded as though he really cared for my honor or something."

"He didn't have your honor in mind."

She tilted her head forward again. "I don't know what he was thinking. All those months in the compound and he never laid a hand on me. I always expected that. At first, I kept thinking of how I could overpower him if he tried to molest me. I knew I couldn't because of my size, but the thoughts kept me going for a while." She swallowed. "Then when I gave up, when I realized that Noah would really hurt Trisha if I tried to leave, and me if he ever caught me, I expected I would just let him…you know…get it over and done with."

Her chin wrinkled and she shut her eyes. And in that moment, he wanted nothing more than to kill his brother. For the torture, for the stress, for everything he'd done to Kaylee.

Lord, what should I do?

She blew out a sigh. "I guess I should be grateful he never touched me, but just standing out there under the deck, he made you sound like you were some evil monster, ready to do exactly as he might do." She gasped, as if hearing her words for the first time. "He made it sound as if you were just like him and he agreed that he was evil!"

"He is."

"But he could have easily killed me that night." She looked queasy. "So why didn't he? Why did he go on like he was you?"

"Noah is an excellent strategist. He's planning something, you can count on it. And part of it includes discrediting me."

Eli shouldn't have spoken. Kaylee paled, looking definitely as if she might throw up. "What could he be planning? To come here pretending to be you? He didn't know I was going to go out on the deck! It was strictly by chance I went out there."

"You went to look at the leash."

"Yes, to see what it was. The wind must have blown it up there."

"Noah put it there to lure you out."

"But he didn't do anything! Eli, I know he's cunning and manipulative, but he could have killed me that night and no one would have known anything until the next day. He lured me out only to tell me that you are as bad as he is. That you're cut from the same cloth."

Cold rippled over him. "He said that?"

"Yes." She frowned. "I think they were the words he used."

Eli pursed his lips. The same words his grandmother used to say when they were playing in her house. He and Noah would get into mischief, mostly of Noah's invention, with him tagging along behind his older brother. But they were both found guilty when the trouble was discovered. Phoebe was just a baby back then and if she was there at the time, she'd have pulled herself up on the playpen slats and watched everything with keen, pale eyes. All Eli's protests of innocence, all Noah's smugness, Phoebe would see them all. Then she'd let out a cry and Noah would go to her, pick her up and tell her it was all Eli's fault.

The words still hurt, he decided after a few moments of thought. His grandmother's complaints were sharp, disapproving and meant to warn his mother to watch both of them. Grandma knew boys. She'd had seven of them, buried three before they could enter school thanks to a fire set by one of them in the old barn, some fifty-odd years ago. She knew boys, all right, and she knew troublesome boys best of all.

Now Noah wasn't just tormenting Kaylee, he was deliberately seeding suspicion in Kaylee. Suspicions that were true.

"Eli?"

He looked at her.

"You're frowning and muttering. What are you thinking?"

"Our grandma used to tell my mother that we were cut from the same cloth. She was very critical of our antics. Of course, Noah was the instigator. It never bothered me when we were young, except when I got into trouble."

"And it hurts now?"

It did, but not because he was remembering his grandmother's criticism. It hurt because it was true. He was as driven as Noah, as callous and pushy, even, determined to have his own way, at any cost. The only difference was that he covered his manipulative nature with a thin veneer of civility. Of Christianity, too.

Lord, why haven't You changed me, like You promised You would in Your Word?

"Eli, *cut from the same cloth* is just an expression and Noah used it to get your goat, as *my* grandmother used to say." She tipped her head to one side to study him. "And Noah knew you would connect the phrase to her and how critical she was. I'm sure Noah let you take the blame for all the mischief."

He smiled softly. "How did you know?"

She grinned. "I was a kid once. This sort of thing isn't just for boys, or even brothers, for that matter. Being accused of doing something you didn't do and getting into trouble for it can scar a kid for life. Just like not owning up to something can haunt a person for life, too. I know that from experience, believe me."

She was trying to make him feel better. It would have worked, too, if the question of what Noah was doing here didn't still linger. He'd had the opportunity to walk right into Kaylee's home. Yes, he toyed with people, planted evil whenever possible. So why suddenly turn pious when the opportunity to hurt her was handed to him on a platter?

Noah was up to something. Out there on that deck. What was it?

Eli spun on his heel and strode out the sliding door. The tiny deck was much like any other found on a house. Kaylee's bungalow was small and the land behind her house dipped sharply. The basement had a walkout door, giving the appearance of a larger, two-story home from the back.

Eli trotted down the deck stairs. As he surveyed the short yard, Kaylee stepped onto the deck.

"What are you doing?" she called down.

"I'm looking for what he might have been up to." He pointed to the back door that led into her basement. "Do you ever use that door?"

She shook her head. "No. The landlord is storing a bunch of old furniture down there. I don't need the basement, so he gave me a cut on the rent, if he uses it as storage. He's actually blocked that door with a huge wardrobe. He said it'll help keep the heat in during the winter."

Eli moved under the deck. He could see some scuffing in the dirt, but nothing clear. One or two marks looked deep, and in front of them, the ground was spotted and the sparse, dormant grass appeared bleached.

He knelt, studying the grass. It was burned. He pulled out a small pocketknife and dug into the soil, then drew the stick up to his nose. The faint smell of rotten eggs.

"What do you see?"

He looked up through the planks of the deck at Kaylee. "I don't know yet. Can you get me some water and baking soda?"

"Baking— Okay." She disappeared into the house

and returned with a two-pound box of soda and a plastic squirt bottle of water. "With Jenn being sensitive to so many chemicals, I've grown used to cleaning with this stuff." She walked down the steps and under the deck.

Eli sprinkled some of the soda onto the patch, and dribbled water on it. The soda fizzled and bubbled slightly.

"What is it?"

"I think it's battery acid. Sulfuric acid, to be precise. Baking soda neutralizes it."

"How did you know what it was?"

"It smelled like rotten eggs. It's a sure sign."

"But how did it get here?" Kaylee looked up and Eli followed her gaze. It was dim under the deck, hard to see, but directly above the patch was the evidence he was looking for.

A section of rotting wood. Straightening, he reached up to nick the soft wood with his knife. It crumbled and danced down to their feet. Taking the soda box again, he sprinkled the white powder onto the flakes. He added water and like the patch of dead ground, it fizzled.

Kaylee gasped. "It's up there, too. The wood is rotten!"

"Not quite. Noah was vandalizing the wood. He was taking his chances, too. This kind of acid can burn when it comes in contact with paper or wood. A spontaneous burn, too, if I remember my chemistry classes. Working with any corrosive chemical is dangerous."

"Where would he have got it, then?"

"Sulfuric acid is used in car batteries. It's easy enough to get a hold of."

"It smells like a match that's just been struck." She

drew in her breath. "Noah had that smell about him. He must have been eating candy to cover it, because he also smelled like sweet mint. I remember now."

They both fell silent with Eli staring up at the wood deck. A candy smell? Had Noah been in the rec center? Why? How did he get in?

It wouldn't be hard to pick the locks. Or slip in and wait until it was closed at night to do laundry, shower, browse the office to read things like Kaylee's schedule…or about the new washer and dryer.

Was this possible? No, he wasn't going to make accusations that could scare Kaylee. Eli poured the water onto the ground and handed her back the small bottle. "Didn't you tell me that your car was acting up?"

"Yes. I think it's the cold weather. It hardly turns over anymore."

"Or the battery's dying because it's lost acid. Do you lock your car?"

She looked sheepish. "I can't. The driver's-door lock is broken. I just don't keep anything valuable in it. No one would want an old junker like that thing."

"No, but someone would like the battery acid, I'd guess. And with the car unlocked, it would be easy to pop the hood." He walked out from under the deck. "We need to call Reading."

"What about the deck? Is it safe to walk on?"

Despite the bright day, under the deck was dark. "I don't know how far he got before you stepped out. We'll have to get a flashlight and check it completely, but I'd say the rain washed away most of the acid before it could do a lot of damage." He pulled out his phone and a small business card.

He watched Kaylee grimace as he dialed. She said,

"I just want to get so mad, to do something now to stop him. He's tormented me for two years and he's still doing it."

She looked at him as he drew the phone up to his ear. "I was ready to fall apart, but not now. If Noah was really using my battery acid, there's got to be proof of that. He wouldn't be carting it around like a bottle of water."

Eli watched her sweep past him and around the house. He followed, only to be delayed when Officer Reading answered his call. Quickly reporting what had been discovered, Eli nodded when Reading told him he'd be there shortly. Hanging up, Eli walked to the front of the house.

Kaylee had already popped the hood of her car and was peering at the battery. "I have no idea what to look for, but it does look as if someone has touched my battery."

Eli leaned over the grille. Several cells of the old battery had seen their caps recently popped off. The green eye in the center of the battery was black, too, a sure sign it had lost cranking power.

"He must have siphoned it off with something," Kaylee said, turning and searching the ground. "And since sulfuric acid is corrosive, he wouldn't want to take it too far."

"Then the container should be here," Eli answered before she moved toward the back of the house again. He liked the determination now sparked in Kaylee. She was fighting back, ready to stop Noah and reclaim her life again. Much better than the denial he'd seen before. But would it last when the truth finally sank in?

They had to find Noah before he killed her.

"Eli!"

FIFTEEN

His heart leaping into his throat, he tore around the bungalow.

Kaylee knelt at the back corner she shared with Lois. Eli caught a glimmer of something in the bushes.

"Here." She pushed away some leggy weeds under a crabapple tree. He came close to peer down. A glass jar with a tight-fitting lid and a syringe. The surrounding ground showed signs of a chemical burn.

Eli searched the area, finding broken branches and scuff marks scaling the ravine. The prints indicated that Noah had moved upstream. "Where does this go to?"

"I'm not sure. I've never followed it. There's a culvert under the road halfway to the motel, then on the other side, I think there's a path through the woods. I'm not sure where it leads."

"The path goes up to the highway. And it connects with the path from downtown that starts by the rec center."

She frowned, a thin veil of suspicion cloaking her expression. "How do you know that?"

"I've checked it out."

"I've never been on it. Jenn told me to avoid it. It's a hangout for teenagers and drunks. I think they have parties there. In the summer, I think they go there to be alone, if you know what I mean."

He did. He'd seen the evidence along the pathway and was glad Kaylee took her boss's advice and avoided it. But he'd had to check it out, see if there could be any evidence that Noah might use it. Hadn't Hec Haines mentioned the trails to Noah?

"So, it's possible that Noah slipped down the ravine, then across to the trail."

"Trails," Kaylee corrected him absently. "They split off in several directions. He could have gone anywhere."

Her voice had turned soft, thoughtful. She stepped back from him and the evidence they'd found. "Noah heading into this corner would have been enough to send Pepe into a frenzy, if he was outside. He must have been here several times."

Eli said nothing, choosing instead to refine the plan he'd formed, to mentally weigh the pros and cons.

"Eli, I don't know how much more I can take! This is crazy! Why is this happening to me? Sure, I said some awful things this past year. I did some things I'm not proud of, but there are others out there that do far worse and their lives are a piece of cake compared to mine. Besides, I had to do those awful things in order to stay alive!"

He listened patiently to her rant. "You're asking me why God lets bad things happen to good people?"

"Yes!" She ran her hands through her hair, a rare gesture for an introvert. "Why?"

She waited for his answer. "Tell me, Eli. Don't walk around the subject like you did at the hospital. I want the straight facts. The ones you believe in. Why does God let awful things happen?"

"To give us a chance to minister to our fellow Christians. To show us that we're not given any more than we can handle. Or perhaps God is preparing us for something greater."

"Greater? Or do you mean worse?"

"It may get worse, but the Lord will be with you if you ask Him to be."

She let out an exasperated noise. "Well, I can't handle any more! I can't handle what I've got now!"

"Why do you say that?"

"Because I can't! Because…"

Calmly, he waited for the rest of her answer. When it didn't come, he asked, "If you couldn't handle it, where would you be?"

Her mouth dropped open and she found herself lost for words. "Dead?"

"I doubt that. Kaylee, you aren't the kind to kill yourself."

"Nor was my sister." She tightened her jaw. "But they said she did it anyway."

"Police are fallible, too. Just remember that you haven't, nor will you ever, be given more than you can handle. God has plans for all of us. And all that happens to us is boot camp for God."

She frowned. "What's that?"

"It's what a pastor friend called any training for His work. Like the army's boot camp."

"Well, I'd get drummed out for sure," she snapped.

Eli knew his expression showed doubt. "I have an idea."

"What?"

He took her arm and guided her into the house. Once inside, he said. "I have a plan, if you're willing."

"What kind of plan?"

"To lure Noah here. He's already been in your yard. He'll be back. He believes he's fooled you."

"He did." She pressed her fingers against her lips, then dropped to the couch.

Eli sat down beside her. "But this time, I'll be outside waiting for him. Officer Reading told me to call him if I thought of a way to help you. Together we could lure Noah out of hiding."

"How?"

"Where are the places you've been lately, that you've announced that you'll be alone? Noah showed up here when you were alone. He tricked you into coming out on the deck."

"That doesn't make any sense. He could have knocked on my door."

"And risk you seeing the difference between us in brighter light? But in the dark, you wouldn't."

"We still don't know why."

"To unnerve you. To toy with you. To play with you or even with me."

She shut her eyes.

Eli barreled on. "How do you think he knew you were alone? Who did you tell?"

"I don't know. You. Some of the people at church may have heard. And we stopped by the rec center so I could pick up my paycheck, but nobody was there yet."

He rose and walked to the phone. Confused, Kaylee just watched him. He called someone, talking softly into the phone for a few minutes. She heard Noah's name, the rec center mentioned and a few words that made no sense. Then she heard him hang up. Returning to the kitchen, he said, "I talked to Reading. I think if you mention that you're home alone at the same places you did last Sunday, we can stake out your house to see if Noah comes."

"So what if he does? We can't do anything about it."

"Reading can arrest him. He's wanted for blowing up his compound." His expression hardened. "We'll get him this time, Kaylee. I promise."

Half an hour later, with his long black flashlight, Reading was peering up at the wood, along with the ground beneath it. Without speaking, Eli handed him the baking soda and water. He'd already mixed them together in a small squirt bottle.

With a squeeze, Reading sprayed the liquid out on the wood. Before dropping to the ground, the milky mixture fizzled and spat. He lifted his eyebrows.

"My kid learned about sulfuric acid in school. Made me nervous, he did. Before I left, I quizzed him on the dangers. It can eat through wood, he said. I remembered they did an experiment on an oak plank. It took a few hours but it rotted it right out."

"And it can spontaneously burn." Eli bit back his impatience. This was Kaylee's deck they were talking about. And if the circumstances had been different, the acid would have eaten right through the wood and she'd have stepped out onto it, to have it collapse under her.

He hadn't mentioned all of this to Kaylee, but he suspected she would guess as much if she sat down to think about it.

Yeah. Despite her show of defiance, she'd ignore it.

"Good thing not much got on the wood—and that we had a big rainstorm to wash it away."

"I'll show you the container we found." He led the officer to the small glass jar. With his pen, Reading lifted the jar and dropped it into a clear plastic bag. "I'll see what I can find out about this."

"I'm sure it's sulfuric acid. Kaylee's battery was dying."

Reading tilted his head. "Someone's been stealing her battery acid?"

"Easiest way to get it. That way, he didn't have to travel far."

"He?"

"Noah. It all points to him."

The officer reflected on Eli's words. They were harsh, judgmental, but he wouldn't temper them when they were talking about Kaylee's safety.

"I'll take this and let you know what I find. I'll take the battery, as well." He swept one last look around the yard before adding, "I'll ask one of the carpenters in town to check your deck out. In the meantime, stay off it."

"Before you go, I have an idea of how to get Noah."

Reading glanced around. "I'm listening."

Two nights later, Eli shifted in the seat of the car Reading had borrowed for him. The cul-de-sac lay quietly before him. Too quiet, he thought irritably.

He sat in the first driveway on the dead-end street, outside the circle of the streetlight. He had an excellent view of Kaylee's house and could see her neighbor, Lois, peeking out of her curtains occasionally. He wished she wouldn't do that, but expected Reading to call her on the phone to tell her so. Reading was located across the street in a small, unlit bungalow. The owners had volunteered to visit family in the city for the night.

Another officer, also a member of the church, watched the other side of the ravine. Two more police officers were on standby.

He scrubbed his face. All they could do now was wait for Noah to show up.

His thoughts moved from the op to the results of the tests on the jar Reading had taken. The police had confirmed it was battery acid, probably taken from Kaylee's battery. The carpenter had come by and recommended two planks and a crossbeam be replaced; the rest would be sealed with a preservative.

But they had nothing, no hair, fingerprints, *nothing* they could pin on Noah.

He hadn't wanted Kaylee to stay alone in the house, but Reading was adamant. If Noah realized a policewoman was there with her, he'd never come. Kaylee agreed.

Just another difficult task he'd dumped on her. Guilt seeped into him and he gritted his teeth to fight it off. He had never intended to put Kaylee through this.

His heart constricted as he realized how much Noah frightened her. How much *he'd* frightened her.

Lord, do something.

He grimaced at his blunt demand. His mind had been on so many details lately that he hadn't spent enough time in prayer, but now, sitting in the car watching her house, he knew he could take the time to pray.

But the words wouldn't form in his head.

Angry with himself, he slumped down and folded his arms. He didn't want anything to happen to Kaylee. He wanted her to stay the way she was and he wanted to capture Noah and, most importantly, find Phoebe. Save her. Take her away and convince her how wrong she was about Noah.

His wants felt hollow—selfish, as Phoebe would say.

Eli stared at the house. Selfish for wanting Phoebe free? Or selfish about Kaylee, not wanting her to change?

Didn't he want Kaylee to change, to accept Jesus as her personal savior? Why would he not want that?

Why?

Because if she accepted Christ, you'd have to admit something you're not prepared to admit, an inner voice whispered. *Something about how you feel about her? Right now, you can keep her at bay, can't you?*

Eli scrubbed his face one more time, hoping to scour away the disturbing thoughts. *Oh, Lord, do something. Now.*

He looked up, bringing Kaylee's small bungalow into focus.

All of a sudden, her home blew apart.

SIXTEEN

Unlike in the woods surrounding the compound, Eli froze.

He gaped at the house as the back portion of it exploded, sending a small fireball into the darkness. Brilliant flames shot into the night sky.

Kaylee! Jolted into action, he scrambled out and he tore down the street. He nearly barreled straight into Reading, who raced from the house across the street. The cop caught Eli at the midpoint and with a tackle, drove him to the ground.

"No! Don't go in there!"

"Kaylee's in there!"

"Wait for the fire department. I just called them."

Lois's front door banged open and the older woman heaved down the front steps. Reading released Eli to intercept her. Eli heard him order her into the house he'd just vacated.

Eli leapt to his feet. The back of Kaylee's home raged with wildfire. *Be with her, Lord, please.*

He couldn't wait for any answer. Ignoring Reading's shouts, he tore up the driveway to her house.

The front door flew open and Kaylee stumbled out.

They met on the lawn. He folded her into his arms. The roar of the fire and the scream of sirens closing in on them drowned out any words she might have said.

Kaylee tilted her head back to peer at the house. In the orange glow, he noticed the welt above her eye. And a gouge forming on her hand as she automatically touched her brow.

He wrapped his left arm around her waist and swung his right one behind her knees to lift her up. Reading was already in the driveway when Eli reached him.

"Is she okay?" the officer barked out.

Eli stared down at Kaylee, his throat clamping off his breath. Then he remembered the cut on her hand. "You're hurt."

"I'm fine. I was walking into the kitchen when…it simply exploded. I think I hit something and…" She blinked and shook her head. "You can put me down."

He set her on the sidewalk across the street from the inferno that had become her house. She tore her eyes away from that sight to ask, "How did I get here? Did you come in?"

"I was on my way in, when you ran out your front door."

"Oh." She glanced over her shoulder at her burning house, as if looking at it like it belonged to some stranger. "Wow. Look at the flames."

Shock, Eli thought. It hasn't sunk in yet. He pulled her tight, tucking her in to hide her face so she couldn't watch. The fire trucks had arrived and behind them with lights also flashing, was the ambulance. Several horrified neighbors had come out of their homes. One couple had hurried into the house Reading had used and were now taking Lois back to their home.

A knot gripped him inside, and he jerked with the sudden pain. Kaylee had nearly died. He'd nearly lost her.

She means a lot to you, a voice within him whispered. *You deserted Phoebe. You deserted Phoebe when you should have gone after her, just to stay with Kaylee.*

She snuggled in close to him and he continued to hold her. So what next? Tell her? Tell her that she meant more to him than Phoebe and then, when all the dust settled around here and they've caught Noah, leave her to go and find his sister?

He couldn't do that to her. She had to deal with too much now. And she was just beginning to explore the faith that had been torn from her so brutally by Noah.

She needed faith more than anything right now.

He clenched his jaw.

She lifted her head. Her hollow look told him the shock was wearing off. "Noah did this."

He fought the anger inside of him. "I know."

"Will they find him?"

"If they don't, I will. I'll stop him."

Pushing him back, she pivoted to stare at the house. "Before it gets any worse?"

Eli handed her a cool wet cloth. "Here." Kaylee took it and set it gingerly against her forehead. It had been hours since the firefighters got the fire under control, but the welt throbbed more now, driving pain across her scalp. "Is a cut supposed to ache this much?"

"I imagine."

She winced as she moved the cloth across her face, following the paramedic's orders and to keep a cool cloth on the bruise now growing on her forehead.

"How could he do this?" she asked, half to herself.

Eli knew who she meant. "Noah's evil, Kaylee. We have to stop him." His voice cracked. "I just can't believe I put your life at risk."

"Don't start blaming yourself," she said. "I agreed to it and Officer Reading approved the plan, too. I'm just not sure how—"

Reading opened the door to the small interrogation room. Another man followed him in. Kaylee recognized the man from the police station in Houlton. Immediately, she felt her shoulders stiffen.

"This is John Wilcox," he introduced. "He's from the Maine State Police. I called him and he asked if he could sit in while we ask you a few questions."

"So you think Noah blew up my house?"

"The preliminary tests indicate that similar explosives were used in both your home and The Farm in Maine. We have no proof yet, but it's good place to start."

She drilled the American with a hard look. "So you'll believe me now when I say that Noah killed my sister?"

"One step at a time. We'd like to find Noah Nash, first."

Reading sat down. Kaylee shifted her chair closer to Eli, to accommodate both men, but Wilcox remained standing.

"I've been sitting in a car for the last three hours," he explained. "I'd rather stand."

"Let's go over what happened," Reading said. "Do you feel up to telling us?"

She nodded. "I'll do my best. But to be honest, I'm not sure I can remember everything. It's all pretty fuzzy and it happened so quickly."

Eli took her hand. "Maybe if we start talking about it, it'll come back to you."

She swallowed. The three men around her waited patiently for her to start, but she couldn't. All she could think about was Noah, trying to kill her.

And these three men wanting to stop him.

Confusion swirled around her. That was good, wasn't it? It had to be done, right? *And yet,* she thought, peeling her hand free, *this is all they want from me.*

To find Noah. Reading and this state police officer, Wilcox, she could understand. They wanted justice, to stop a madman and keep Riverline, and her, safe.

But what about Eli?

He wanted to find Phoebe. And he wanted revenge on Noah for taking her. He'd get it at any cost.

Kaylee shivered.

Eli leaned forward. "Do you need more time?"

She bit her lip, afraid to face the hurt forming in her heart. He said he was a Christian, a man who wanted to follow his Lord, but did that include putting her life at risk? Yes, the explosion shocked him, but before that, did he really think she was expendable? Noah had considered others expendable, even Trisha. Phoebe had once said those not chosen by Noah had to die when the world ended.

Did that attitude run in the family?

And what about justice for Trisha?

"I can't." She rocketed out of her chair and turned away from the men. "I don't remember! I don't know what to say!"

Eli and Reading leaned back in their chairs and all three men let out a collective sigh that bore a frustrated note.

She spun around to glare at them. "I don't remember, okay? It's hard. And I keep thinking of Trisha. Noah killed her and the police didn't do anything about it. They believed Noah over me." She heard her voice start to rise. "How do I know you'd believe me now? Sure, you're starting at an obvious place, Noah, but what guarantees do I have that you'll stick with him as the main suspcct? What about justice for Trisha? People think she committed suicide! That's not fair to her."

Reading rose, but she caught a glimpse of Eli holding out his hand to stop him. Eli was the one who spoke. "Give us a couple of minutes, will you?"

The two men left her alone with him. She stood staring at a small poster that listed some basic human rights in three languages. English, French and an aboriginal language she didn't recognize. Her head hurt, she felt grimy and her stomach growled. And now the room smelled stuffy and hot.

"Kaylee, I know where you're coming from."

She turned to him. "Do you?"

"I do. It's frustrating when no one believes you and you know you're right."

"And when has that happened to you?" she asked dryly.

"When Noah graduated high school and was working for John, our cousin, I knew something wasn't right. They spent a summer together doing some truck driving and when they returned, things were different with him. Noah was suddenly interested in things he hadn't been before."

"Like what?"

Eli rose. "He started to check out things like different kinds of security, weapons, even explosives. He started to talk about the military. Our father just said he was trying to decide what to do with his life. Dad wouldn't have minded if he'd enlisted, but I knew Noah wasn't going to take orders from anyone. However, whenever I brought the subject up, no one would believe me."

They were getting off-track here and Kaylee didn't want to hear about Noah's younger years or how he began his reign of manipulation and evil. "Eli, I appreciate what you're trying to say here. Your parents couldn't bring themselves to believe that Noah would go bad, but that's not the real point here. I *don't* think I can help anyone. I don't remember what happened."

"You need to tell them exactly what you *do* remember. These men are trained to ask the right questions. They can help you."

"There's nothing to say."

He pursed his lips. With a careful step forward, he searched her face. "There's more, isn't there?"

"No."

"It's about me, isn't it?"

She turned away.

"Answer me, Kaylee. Is this about me?"

Even small movements stabbed pain into her forehead so she stayed dead still. Why weren't those pain-killers working?

"Kaylee? What's going on?"

She couldn't answer him. Answering meant admitting that she cared for him and that he would hurt her when he left. And regardless of what he might say, Eli was planning to leave.

He ran his hand over his face. "We've got to find Noah. You know that."

A hard lump formed in her throat. "I know."

"And you *can* help with that."

"So you can find Noah." Inside of her swirled hot emotions—fear, anger, hurt. But she needed all those feelings to stay in check or else they'd spill out and hurt both of them.

It took her a few minutes before she realized that Eli hadn't said anything. She dared a painful look at him, finding that same odd, frowning expression he wore after he'd carried her off her lawn. Were the same swirls of emotions inside him? For a moment, she considered reaching forward to smooth away the frown.

But she'd only be torturing herself further.

"So I can find Noah, yes." Eli finally said. "Is that it? You don't want me to find him?" He shook his head in disbelief. "You're not still thinking Noah's this world's savior, are you?"

"No!" Her eyes widened. "I know he's not! I know that what he thinks and what all of them think of him is wrong! He's evil, plain and simple." She clamped her mouth shut. Oh, did she have to spell it all out? Did he have to force her to admit that she cared for him?

Wetting her lips, she sat down again. Eli bent his knee to come to eye level. He looked as if he wanted to say something, too, but was holding back.

Kaylee felt her insides clench. "Say it. Tell me I'm wrong for not being more helpful to Officer Reading."

"You're not wrong. You're confused and upset and no one will blame you for not wanting to talk right now."

"Then what do you want to say? I know you have more than that on your mind."

He didn't say anything. And she couldn't read his answer in his eyes. Finally, he took her hands in his. "Let's pray."

She wanted to tug back her fingers, but remembered the conviction Lois once mentioned. God would want her to help the police, not protect her selfish emotions.

Before, yes, she'd felt convicted and helped Eli. Now, her house gone, her life a mess—

As if sensing her animosity, Eli gripped her hands tighter. "Kaylee, for me, please? Let me pray. You can just listen."

He prayed. She watched his bowed head until guilt told her to close her own eyes. There was no sense of the peace that was supposed to come with prayer. All she could think of was how much God must hate her for the things she'd been forced to say and the things she'd eventually thought and the things she refused to do now.

Yet, Eli's soft words did make her feel a bit better. Still just as sad, still just as worried for what would eventually happen, but she did feel a little better.

He lifted his head when he ended the prayer. "We'll find Noah, I promise."

She freed her hands. *And what then,* she wondered? *How long will it be before you leave?* She should leave first. That way, it wouldn't hurt as much. That way, she could stop Eli from using her as bait. And doing those things that Christians shouldn't do.

"Eli?"

He glanced up at her. "Yes?"

Claiming that she was stopping him from doing sinful things was just an excuse to cover the truth she didn't want to admit.

She couldn't fool Eli. "Nothing. I—I'm ready to help now."

The door swung open and in walked Reading and Wilcox. Each man wore a grim expression. Reading spoke. "The fire department just called."

Her house was totaled, she thought. Gone, and there was no reason for her to stay. Another reason to leave Riverline. A good solid excuse this time.

"And?" Eli prompted.

Reading cleared his throat. "They found a body in the kitchen. It's badly burned, not recognizable at all. But from the preliminary exam, the coroner says it was male, about the same height and weight as Noah Nash."

SEVENTEEN

Relief drenched her. She heaved out a much-needed sigh and felt her shoulders droop.

Beside her, Eli went rigid, cool. "Are you sure?"

Reading lifted his eyebrows, his grim expression changing to uncertainty. "Not sure, yet. The coroner is taking the body down to Fredericton for an autopsy. What you can do to help prove it's Noah is to give a sample of your DNA. We can match it, if you both have the same parents."

"We do. Where do I go to give a DNA sample?"

"We'll make the arrangements for a mouth swab."

"How long will it take to find out for sure?"

Reading shrugged. "Local DNA analyses are done in Halifax. But it could take weeks to confirm it. I'll see what I can do to speed things up."

Eli's expression turned as grim as Reading's had become. Kaylee stood. "But it's a good chance that it was Noah, right?"

"Yes."

Reading's statement confirmed it for Kaylee. She drew in her breath. With Noah dead, there was no need for Eli to stick around. She may as well get the rest of the difficult stuff over with. It was better than brooding on things that could never be. She looked at Reading. "You wanted to interview me? I'll do my best this time."

They all sat down. She began. "I was sitting in my living room, flicking through the TV channels. It must have been the top of the hour because the shows were starting. That's when I first heard a noise."

Reading leaned forward. "What kind of a noise?"

She shook her head. "I don't know. A clicking sort of noise, but not like the back door opening or closing. That door squeaks. This was more like electronic clicks."

"Where did they come from?"

"The kitchen. I thought at first that I should call you. Or Eli."

Reading wore a question on his face. "You didn't call me."

Eli shook his head. "You didn't call me, either."

"No," she corrected. "Then I thought that it might have been the refrigerator making noise because the back door didn't open. I was alone. Or so I thought."

"What happened next?"

She grimaced. "Someone was there in the kitchen. I think whoever it was had been hiding in the house."

Eli shot a frown toward Reading. Kaylee easily guessed the men's thoughts. For the last day, they'd let it be known she'd be alone tonight. They should have cleared the house first. Was it even procedure to do so? She didn't know. Nor did she want to point out such an obvious error in case they hadn't done it. These men already knew what should have been done.

Too late to be concerned about that.

"I remember walking into the kitchen and seeing movement—" She stopped, realizing she didn't know what happened next.

Frustrated by the sudden gap in her memory, she sat back.

"The electronic clicks, then—" she whispered, tucking an errant strand of hair behind her right ear.

Eli leaned over. "You heard them again?"

She tunneled her hair with her fingers, cringing when she brushed against the scrape on her forehead. "Arg! This is crazy." She looked up, blankly. "I should be able to remember."

Eli was about to answer when Wilcox spoke. "You heard the clicks, then walked into the kitchen. Close your eyes, picture it in your head."

She tried. "I don't remember." Stricken, she searched the men's faces. "Wait! I heard the clicks the first time, then again after I'd listened for a bit, *then* I walked into the kitchen, saw him—"

"Him?"

She blinked. "I think it was a him. Tall, slim, a blur, really. I—" She sank back in her seat again. "I'm sorry. I remember something blue and…"

Reading leaned over. "And what?"

"The next thing I remember, I was outside. Eli was carrying me." She let out a frustrated noise. "Blue?"

"What was blue?" Eli asked.

She perused his clothing. They all smelled slightly of smoke and some chemicals, probably the result of her house burning. But Eli wasn't wearing blue. He had on a tan-colored shirt and dark green pants.

"Have you been wearing that all evening?"

He cast a look down at his clothing. "Just this with my light green jacket."

"Do you remember what Noah was wearing when you saw him in the backyard?" Reading asked.

She pressed her lips into a thin line, then brightened. "Blue! He was wearing blue!"

Reading smiled. "Good. Now, do you remember how you hurt yourself? What you hit to make those marks? Was it soft, rounded, hard, pointed?"

"Hard. I think I hit the corner of the wall where the front hall meets the living room."

"Do you remember thinking that you were going to fall? Or reaching out to stop yourself? Do you remember being scared?"

"Yes! I was scared. I remember the wall and thinking I was going to hit it! I pushed out my arms and then I hit the floor. Yes, I turned quickly. It's a laminate floor and it's slippery." She smiled, thankful something was coming back to her. "That's how I hurt my hand. I tried to catch myself, but I ended up hitting my head on the wall and my hands on the floor by the corner."

Reading found a slip of paper and a pen. "Draw a plan of your house. Show me where the wall is in relation to the kitchen."

She took the pen. Her hand shook as she sketched out his request. The front door led straight down the hall into the kitchen. The wall on the right ended a few feet past the front door. "There's this old mat. I remember thinking it had moved away from the door. It always does. I slipped on the mat and went headfirst into the wall."

"Which means you were running away from the kitchen."

Amazed, she nodded to Reading. He was good at coaxing out information. "Yes. I must have been. I saw something that scared me. It had to be Noah. There isn't anyone else who would have me tearing to the front door." She thought hard for a moment. "But that's all I can remember, I'm afraid."

Reading reached to pat her hand. "You did very well. Sometimes we need time to process a traumatic experience before we can recall it. We can try again later."

He stood, along with Wilcox and Eli. Wearily, she rose, too. "Can I see my house? Can I even stay there?"

With sympathy, Reading shook his head. "I'm afraid not. Not only is it a crime scene, but it's probably going to be condemned." He checked the time on his wristwatch. "Later this morning, you may be allowed to retrieve some things, but I suggest, since it's after midnight, you find another place to stay."

"Another place?" She looked blankly around until his words sunk in. "I suppose Lois may be able to put me up for a few days…."

Reading answered with another shake of his head. "Her house sustained some damage, as well. The fire inspector will have to check it out before she's allowed back in. She's gone over to our place. My wife came and got her a few hours ago."

"You can stay up in the motel." Eli looked at Reading. "It has good security."

Reading agreed. "Yes. It's a good place. The owner just renovated and changed all the locks. He installed some security cameras, as well. I can get him out of bed to get you a room, if you like."

“Thank you.” She watched him and Wilcox leave. It felt so unreal. Not like a dream, but part of an illusion, a daydream gone crazy. Sometimes while she was trapped at The Farm, she would fall into musing of things that she could have been doing, except they would invariably lead to sadness. The same sensation lingered today.

Eli took her arm and she let him lead her out of the tiny room. His grip was firm, comforting in a way, but she felt too stiff and robotic to move fluidly with him.

Reading caught up with them at the station’s front door. “Mr. Nash, I’ve got someone to take that DNA sample now.”

Kaylee tried to focus on the conversation. Reading stood beside another officer. That man held a long cotton swab in his hand. Eli nodded and opened his mouth.

The man swabbed in the inside of Eli’s cheek. Over and over again, it seemed. They wanted a good sample. They wanted proof that it was Noah in that fire.

When the officer was finished, Eli took Kaylee’s elbow again.

They drove to the motel in silence. As they arrived, the owner was just unlocking his office door. He offered his condolences and even promised to keep the reporters away from her if she liked.

She tried to register for the room, but her hand shook too much to write. The owner took the pen, saying that she could finish filling out the registration later. With a grateful nod, she thanked him.

Eli dug out his wallet, the same battered leather she’d seen that first day they’d met. He handed the owner his credit card for the man to take a swipe.

Outside, she thanked him. "I don't have a credit card yet, but I'll get you the money. I promise."

"Forget it. All I want you to do is sleep." He walked down the strip of rooms to stop at hers, and unlocked her door. After turning on the main light, he handed her the key. "My room's two doors down. Call me if you need anything."

She blinked. "I don't even have a toothbrush."

He smiled. "We can worry about those details later today. Just remember, Kaylee, you're okay. All that was lost were just things." He gave her hand a squeeze.

As if it snapped her out of her confusion, she held his hand firmly. "I guess I still need to process this. I'm sorry I haven't been much help tonight. I was downright nasty to you back at the police station."

He rubbed his face. "You weren't nasty. You were being honest. It was me who wasn't."

"No, that's not true." She shut the door to keep the heat in. The night, while not as cold as it could be, chilled her. The jacket she wore was borrowed from the neighbor across the street. It hung on her frame and offered little insulation. She drew it closer to her.

"Kaylee," he began before she could speak, "everything you did was understandable. And I wish I could say the right thing to make you feel better and help you help the police. But I couldn't. That's why I prayed."

It helped, she thought. But apart from a little peace, what else could it give her? Eli needed to find Phoebe; God would approve of that. Any prayer to Him she might say would only be to ask Eli to stay and that would hardly be God-consented, right?

It wasn't going to happen anyway. "Well, thank

you for all you've done. It's over now. Noah is dead and…and I'm dead on my feet."

"Take those painkillers. I'll check on you after lunch."

He didn't move. A crease formed between his brows and his mouth opened slightly. A second later, he bent down and touched his lips to her cheek. A part of her wanted to cling to him, but he lifted his head too soon for her to react. She offered him a brief twitch of her lips and pushed open the door behind her. Without another look back, she bowed her head and closed the door.

Lord, give her a good night's sleep. Give her peace and strength. After his hasty prayer, he strode quickly down to his room.

He stopped at the door and found his attention sliding along the cool frontage to Kaylee's room.

Would she sleep soundly? He'd once heard a pastor say that God relentlessly pursues those fighting the leading of the Spirit. The only relief they got was sleep and, like wild children, they slept soundly.

Noah used to sleep well, like the dead, their mother would say. A scoundrel during the day, a baby at night.

Her words were loving, long before he took her daughter and disappeared, leaving her deeply hurt.

Did Noah still sleep soundly? Probably and probably only a few hours a night. In some of the training he'd taken while working for the police force, he learned about the psyche of people like Noah. They slept well, though only briefly, and thrived on this routine.

Eli stood silently for several minutes, his key still in his left hand, his right one lightly resting on the door handle to his room.

Did Kaylee also sleep well? Was it her only peace from the Lord's constant pursuit?

Suddenly unwilling to hear an answer, he thrust the key into the lock and plowed inside.

The next morning came too early for him. A quick glance to the digital clock and some mental math told him he'd only managed four hours' sleep. He'd laid awake for at least an hour, praying, mulling over his brother's death. Trying to sort out his reaction to it. Only after realizing no reaction was coming, did he fall asleep.

Something had awoken him. It was a light knock on the door, he realized. Tossing off the covers he called out, "Just a sec."

Hastily dressed, he opened the door. Kaylee stood there. She looked tired, resigned almost.

"Sorry for getting you up so early, but Reading called. A patient had to be air-evacuated to the Halifax Infirmary, and they sent yours and Noah's DNA down with him. A technician was able to tell something about the mitochondrial DNA—they're both the same."

He stifled a yawn and nodded to himself. "Mitochondrial DNA is passed down from mothers to their children. That means it's Noah."

There lingered a long pause as both absorbed what it really meant. Finally, Kaylee added, "I also wanted to let you know that I'm going to walk down to the house. To see if I can get in and get some things I need." She shrugged. "If there's anything worth salvaging. The fire department called me this morning to say that the fire inspector is on his way."

"You won't be allowed in. They won't risk your

safety or the security of the scene. It's a crime scene, now. What did you need?"

Her expression turned vague. "Clothes, if I have any left, and maybe some toiletries. I know they can be replaced, but only if you have money. Which I don't."

"They'll probably only let you in for prescription medicines."

She sighed, pulling up on the borrowed jacket's collar. "I thought you would want to know where I was. Go back to bed. You look as tired as I feel."

"No." He pivoted, grabbed his jacket and followed her out. "We'll take the car. I don't feel like walking and I imagine you don't, either."

He shot her a sidelong look as he slipped on his jacket. "How did you sleep?"

"Better than I expected."

He shouldn't have asked. Her answer wasn't what he wanted to hear. Fishing out his keys, he led her to his car. All the way to her house, he tried to force her answer from his mind. Should he be getting involved with a woman who fought God's interference in her life so constantly?

The smell of smoke permeated the car even before they reached Kaylee's cul-de-sac. In the stark morning light, the house looked irreparable. Kaylee let out a soft moan.

Then they noticed the TV crew from a station that reported all the news in the Maritimes. Eli parked down the street a bit. Several neighbors hovered a safe distance away and half a dozen or so kids had gravitated closer to the camera. An elderly man was being interviewed.

"Let's wait here. Maybe the news crew will leave without seeing us."

"You have New York license plates, Eli."

"But they may not notice us. Let's pray they have enough of a story."

"I didn't see them last night," Kaylee mused.

"They may have only found out this morning."

Finally, the interview ended and the crew climbed into their van and drove off. Hulking down, Eli and Kaylee watched a tall woman with blond hair drag on her seat belt as they drove past. "I've seen her on TV," Kaylee mused.

"Safe to get out now."

The bright yellow police tape cordoned off the entire lot, and Lois's, as well. Kaylee's house looked as if a giant torch had crushed down on one side of it. The other half appeared normal, but Eli knew that the brick exterior would be cracked, the mortar pitted and no longer waterproof. Most likely, the house would have to be torn down.

Reading spotted them from inside the tape and after flipping up the yellow plastic, he strode toward them. "It's not looking good inside," he said. "A lot of water damage. There's nothing left for you to salvage."

Kaylee blinked. "That's all right. I didn't have much. My aunt has most of my stuff." Her gaze wandered to Lois's house. "What about hers?"

He shook his head. "We haven't been in to look yet. Aunt Lois wanted to come by earlier, but my wife convinced her to go back to bed. Her house seems to have sustained some heat and smoke damage and my wife didn't want her inhaling any of it."

"Wise."

"Her insurance-company adjuster was here earlier. He said you have a policy with him, too."

She nodded. "I forgot completely about that. Yes, just a renter's policy. And not for very much."

"He said he'll be back. I know him. He's good at helping people. I told him where he could reach you, both at the motel and at your work." Reading looked up at Eli. "I assume you heard about the test?"

"Yes."

"The coroner ordered a more complete DNA analysis plus a tox screen and blood tests. We've fast tracked this case, so it could take as little as a day or two."

"Do you think Noah was under the influence of drugs?"

Reading shrugged. "Possibly, or perhaps there was something medically wrong. It's part of the autopsy. We've also had the explosive experts in and they've taken their samples, too." He turned to Kaylee. "The building inspector's here now. It doesn't look good."

Tears filled her eyes. Reading reached out to take her hand. "The guy who did this is dead, Kaylee. That's one thing we can be thankful for. He won't be hurting you again. And this is just a house—a house that can be replaced."

She took back her hand and pulled her jacket closer around her. "I know. But just when I was getting my life together, this happens. I don't know how much more I can take."

Eli bit back his answer. This was not the time for a sermon. He'd be doing more damage than good. Instead, he offered up a silent prayer.

When another officer called Reading over, he left. Kaylee remained staring at the blackened brick and charred roof trusses. "Noah's gone. And you'll have to tell Phoebe." He heard her draw in a long breath that had a shaky edge to it. "So when do you leave?"

EIGHTEEN

I must really love to torture myself, Kaylee decided as soon as the words left her mouth. Why else would she ask Eli such a painful question?

And with Eli's frown deepening, she wasn't even sure she wanted to hear the answer. Her heart seemed to stall as if she stood on a precipice, both wanting and not wanting to fall over the edge.

"I'm still waiting for my investigator to get back to me with a photo." He paused, shooting a scowl at the remains of her house. "Plus, I want to wait for the results of the DNA test."

An excuse? she wondered. Did it matter, anyway? He was still leaving. "It was him. I can feel it. The same feeling I had at The Farm."

His blond lashes hooded his eyes. "It's not me I want to satisfy."

"Phoebe? You don't think she'll believe you?"

"I don't know. It's been seven years since I saw her. And who knows what Noah's been feeding her all that time."

"I know. I was also feeding her lies near the end." She shut her eyes. "But only during prayer vigils. Eli, they're such fools. I'm glad Noah's gone, as unchristian as that sounds. After each vigil, Phoebe used to tell me that I had such a wonderful gift. She refused to remember that I was being kept against my will." She cringed inwardly. Was she trying to convince him that going to Phoebe was a mistake? How could she be so cruel?

"Then how did Noah convince them that you were genuine? I mean, there must have been some opposition, especially after you kept telling them you were being held against your will."

She opened her eyes. "Remember I told you that some women asked Noah to get rid of me? Phoebe wasn't one of them. Noah told her that I was fighting my natural gift of prophecy, and that it was the evil in me, that God was telling him to save me."

Though the memory didn't hurt as much now, she still found herself biting her lip as she finished. "When I got scared that he was going to hurt me, or worse, I just obeyed him, kept quiet and did my best."

"And the opportunity to escape never arose?"

"No." When a cool breeze drifted in, she hugged herself. "I was watched all the time. Normally, I like to be alone, so you can imagine how awful that was. Trisha pleaded with me to give the cult a try. Phoebe told me I had natural gifts and the sin in me was fighting them.

"After Noah threatened me that one time in the basement, I got really scared and tried my best to do what he said." She stared at him. "I would cry through the prayers and Noah told everyone that was good, that it meant I was being cleansed and the truth was finally being freed." With a wash of sudden embarrassment, she turned away.

He touched her shoulder. "Don't say any more. I know it hurts."

She turned, shaking her head. "Yes, it does, but you know what? It's getting easier to talk about it. Besides, I don't want to dwell on what's just happened. Noah's dead. It's all over."

"Kaylee, you should—"

She ignored him and kept on talking. "I figured that if I did a good job at prophesying, Noah would stop his threats. Each day that he held those prayer vigils, he'd coach me. I was terrified, not to mention hungry and tired. Sometimes, if I did a good job and didn't mess up, he'd give me a reward, like a sandwich or something."

The memory was humiliating, yes, but when she relived those events, like the way she wolfed down those thin sandwiches ravenously, she didn't have to focus on the house that could have been her tomb.

Eli slid his hand down to meet hers, something she liked very much. He felt wonderfully warm. "Whatever happened there was not your fault. And if Phoebe doesn't believe me about Noah, it won't be your fault, either. Or mine. I just want to provide her with the irrefutable proof that he's dead, along with the proof of what he did to you."

He steered her to face the house. "Don't force yourself to relive old pains because the present pain is too hard. Don't live as a victim of your own bad circumstances. Face what's happening. It'll help you to deal with it. God can help you, you know? All you have to do is ask." His fingers tightened around her hands.

She couldn't say anything. Was he right? If God was so kind, why did He let her suffer so much in the first place? Would He really help her, if she just asked? Hadn't she been asking before? Had she been asking for the wrong things?

Only empty silence answered. She shoved the questions aside. "You should be getting the proof you say you need, instead of helping me. I'm coping the best way I know how."

"Do you think Phoebe will accept my word alone?"

Her heart leaped. Was he thinking of leaving right away? "No," she answered. "No, she won't. She believes so totally in Noah's vision of the future and that he's chosen by God that you won't convince her with just your word."

"No one ever mentioned me? Phoebe? John? Noah?"

He shouldn't ask her that. It would hurt him too much if they talked about it. She glanced up at him, her answer obvious on her face.

He lowered his eyes. "I'm sorry. I just thought someone might have."

She bit her lip. "No, and I know why. Phoebe wouldn't talk about you because you didn't share their vision of the future. Of course, we didn't share a lot of small talk. She would get chatty now and then, mostly in the evening during the summer, when the upstairs was hot and we'd have to open the living-room window. When I was allowed downstairs. There was no screen, so we'd keep the window open only until the mosquitoes started to come in."

"What would she talk about?"

"Mostly she'd talk about the new world they were preparing for. There would be no bugs in it. The weather would be perfect. And there wouldn't be any night."

"What else would she say?"

"She said that Noah was chosen to prepare for this new world and he could choose who he wanted for it, like Peter was allowed to choose who gets into Heaven." She gently tugged her hands free of his and rubbed her forehead, feeling another headache move in.

"Did Phoebe hurt you?"

"Only with her words. She'd say I should be honored to have been chosen. That life wasn't just about material wealth and possessions, but about the journey we take, the way we react to trouble."

"How did that hurt you?"

"Try to understand something. I was confused. It hurt when she suggested I was materialistic and selfish. She was always calling me selfish."

Pain flickered over his face. She longed to know his thoughts. But sharing such intimate details would make the inevitable break that much harder. She was barely hanging on with her own pain, he didn't want to add more to it. But was she as selfish as Phoebe accused her of being?

No, she wasn't. Nor should she let one misguided woman tell her so. Not wanting to be hurt wasn't being selfish.

They stood in the sunshine, the cool wind drifting the stench of charred wood and brick over their faces. To prove to herself that she wasn't selfish, Kaylee said, "You should go as soon as you can."

He stiffened. "Yes."

"Go, then. Get a head start, especially if you plan to drive to Florida. Reading can send you the proof you'll need."

His expression changed, became more pensive. She swallowed. Oh, mercy, he was actually considering it.

Suddenly, the moment peaked, and she tore her gaze free. He *was* going to leave. He was actually planning the trip in his mind at that moment.

The cold breeze changed direction and she turned away from the house. "I should go down to the rec center. I have to work today."

Eli didn't answer and she didn't steal a glance to see what he might be thinking. Instead, she walked past his car and toward the road that led into town.

And as much as it hurt her, Eli didn't follow, nor did he call out an offer to drive her down.

It's okay, she told herself. She needed to walk and he realized that. It was safe for her walk alone now, and Eli would see she needed to release her nervous energy.

She picked up her pace.

As soon as she entered the rec center, she saw the boxes stacked along the wall. Hearing the door open, Jenn poked her head out of the office.

"They're for you," she said, indicating the boxes.

Curious, Kaylee knelt down in front of the nearest one. "What's in them?"

"I don't know. All I know is that some of your church members dropped them by a few minutes ago. Open them."

Most of the sturdy boxes were scrounged from the local grocery store. She opened the biggest one. Inside was a pot set.

The next one had brand-new bedding and towels. Another had canned and dried foodstuffs. Kaylee looked up at Jenn, blankly. "For me?"

"Your church heard about the fire. Your pastor came by with Hec Haines. That was when I first found out about it. Was anyone hurt? You should have called me!"

"I'm fine, surprisingly. No smoke inhalation or burns or anything." She wet her lips. "But there was a body found in the house."

Jenn gasped. "Who was it?"

"Noah Nash."

"The guy who kidnapped you? He was here? Oh, Kaylee, how awful!" She let out a much-relieved sigh. "I don't know how you've managed."

"I don't feel like I have."

Watching Jenn rise and carry one of the boxes into the office, Kaylee grimaced. "I should call my aunt. She'll hear of the fire pretty soon." The local TV crew had already come and gone. It would be reported on the noon news, something her aunt never failed to watch.

"Use the office's phone," Jenn invited, returning to retrieve another box.

"Thanks." Grabbing a box, she followed her boss into the office and quickly dialed the familiar number.

Her aunt's voice sounded wonderful, Kaylee thought. She hadn't heard of the fire, yet, but to her credit, though, she didn't fret and cry. She listened carefully to all the details that Kaylee gave her. Her only words were, "Come home, dear. We miss you. I ran into a few of your friends yesterday and they want to see you. They're good friends and want to help you. We all do."

An alluring wash of homesickness warmed her. She should go home. She should face the questions and clear up the rumors about Trisha. Maybe it was time.

And Eli? She couldn't exactly drag him along, not with the trip to her hometown taking him farther away from Florida.

He needed to go there.

"I need to stay here a few more days to sort some things out," she told her aunt. "I'll call you again, okay?" After hanging up, Kaylee turned to Jenn, who was furtively poking into the boxes, obviously curious.

"What's in the rest of them?" she asked her.

Hastily, Jenn shut the one box. "Mostly stuff you'll need to get your life started again. One box has some clothes and another has toiletries and one even has a phone. They've thought of everything. How sweet!"

Tears stung Kaylee's eyes as she dug into the boxes herself. Lois's church cared. They were doing God's work, like Eli had said. Not for salvation, but for love of Him. Did that mean that they were her church, too?

She slammed shut the one box. Jenn peered across at her inquiringly. "I have to find a place to stay before I can use any of this stuff," she explained.

"Where did you stay last night? Don't tell me you stayed up!"

Kaylee shook her head. "I went to the motel."

"With Eli?" Jenn's eyebrows shot up.

Despite everything, Kaylee laughed. "No! I mean, he drove me up there. I had my own room. Get your mind out of the gutter, Jenn."

Jenn shrugged. "I didn't mean for it to go there. It's just that he cares for you. Everyone can see that. I was only wondering how far he'd take it. It must be hard on you, he being Noah's brother and all. He's got to remind you of Noah..." Her words died away and she cleared her throat. "Listen to me ramble. Sorry."

Sobering now, Kaylee gave her boss a stern look. Yet underneath, the questions Jenn raised lingered. Did Eli care for her? Was this *thing* they were sharing getting personal for him, too? One thing she was sure of was that she no longer thought of Noah when she looked at Eli. She thought of Eli, of how much she was starting to care for him.

It wasn't going to lead anywhere. And as a Christian, he would choose to save himself for marriage to a nice girl who shared his faith. Kaylee knew that much. Pastor Paul had delivered a message on that theme at last week's sermon.

And Eli was sensible enough to know his time in her life was brief, only for a season. They both knew it.

But it hurt.

Thrusting away the thought, she stacked the boxes in the far corner. "Can I store these here for a few days, until I find another place?"

"Of course. And if you need any time off, just say so. In fact," Jenn said as she rose to scoop up a candy wrapper that had drifted to the floor with the draft Kaylee created. "I can clean up for a few days. It won't kill me. I'm planning to chase those kids out the next time I catch them in here. I think they're sneaking in here when I have to leave the office for something. I've lost my scissors, papers have moved. I'm going to start supergluing everything to my desk."

Kaylee watched her thrust her fists against her waist. Jenn took care of all the paperwork, and worked hard, but she didn't see half the messes and mischief the teenagers got into. Perhaps she was just lightening the moment with humor. It didn't matter. She appreciated her boss's attempts to keep her spirits up.

"Thanks, but I'd like to work for a bit. You know, something to keep me busy? The insurance agent is supposed to call."

"Whatever you think is best. There's some sweeping needed in the hall."

Kaylee started her work. The hall smelled of the candy being made next door. The smell of butter and caramel and fresh mint teased her stomach into growling. She hadn't eaten yet today. When she first arrived in Riverline, the doctor had warned her to eat at least three light, bland meals each day, giving her a sample menu to follow. It didn't include candy, but now, the sweet smell tempted her.

The morning and most of the afternoon flew by and Kaylee was already done most of her tasks when Eli walked in.

Her heart skipped at the sight of him filling the front doorway. Oh, yes, she thought only of Eli. Him and him alone.

Another danger, for sure.

Wearing a firm expression, he stepped into the building. "I should have asked you if you wanted a ride to work."

"It's all right. I needed to walk."

"Did you eat breakfast?"

"I wasn't hungry."

"I hope you are now. I stopped by the deli and got them to make up a couple of meals for us. Can you take a late lunch break?"

She glanced at Jenn, who peered out through the

glass window, her eyes lit with almost comical interest. “I don’t think Jenn would mind. Smelling the store next door all day has made my stomach growl. They must be cooking up another batch of candy.”

Eli sniffed the air, but said nothing.

He was preoccupied. Thinking of a way to say goodbye?

Just say it, her heart cried out. Or better still, her head suggested, just leave when she wasn’t around.

Jenn was already at the door to the office, one of the boxes in her hand. “This one has the toiletries and some clothes in it. You’ll probably need these at the motel.” With a long sweeping look up Eli’s frame, she handed him the box. “Could you take this for Kaylee?”

Eli agreed and they walked outside to his car. “Sorry about that,” she said. “It’s just Jenn’s way. She must be a romantic at heart.”

He frowned. “What do you mean?”

She pinkened, realizing that an explanation would embarrass them both. Jenn wanted to get them together, and Kaylee refused to put that kind of pressure on either of them. She struggled to find another answer. “Jenn asking you to take that box.”

He smiled. “I don’t mind carrying it, Kaylee.”

They drove to the motel. She dug out her key and Eli brought the box inside while she carried in the meals and set them out on the small table. They ate in an uncomfortable, difficult silence.

A whirring suddenly cut through the air, making Kaylee jump.

“My cell,” Eli explained. He pulled it out and answered it.

It wasn’t hard to realize it was Officer Reading on

the line. Eli listened carefully, a frown deepening with each passing moment.

Dread washed over her. More bad news? Phoebe? Had something happened to her?

Kaylee bated her breath, still gripping the small carton of milk Eli had bought for her.

This nightmare was over, right?

Finally, Eli hung up.

She waited as he tucked his cell phone back into his shirt pocket. "Well?" she blurted out. "What happened?"

"The DNA tests came back."

"And?"

"Yes, the mitochondria matched."

Relief washed over her. "Just as Officer Reading said. It *was* Noah."

"No. Mitochondrial DNA would match, but they have the other results." Eli shook his head, shoved back his chair and stood. "They did a full DNA comparison, just as the coroner wanted. The results show there wasn't the match siblings would have. It wasn't Noah who died. It was John."

NINETEEN

"But the DNA matched! They told us!"

Eli heard the alarm in her voice and kept his own calm. "The mitochondrial DNA matched. You see, Noah and I have the same mother, but John's mother and my mother are sisters, so John has the same mitochondria, too. We share a maternal grandmother."

Kaylee flew to standing, drawing her hands up to her temples and pressing against them with her fingertips. "This is insane! He's insane! He'd kill his own flesh and blood to exact revenge on me."

"I know, he's crazy, Kaylee. At least now, we can get the police to—"

"To what? They've been looking for him all along!" Then, as if she just realized the full measure of his words, her eyes widened.

"We?" She shook her head vigorously and held up her hand. "Oh, no, you can. I'm done here." She stalked over to the box he'd brought in.

He twisted around. "What are you doing?"

"I'm going home."

"Home?"

"Yes, to Nova Scotia."

"Kaylee—"

"No, I have an aunt who wants me to visit. I have friends who are worried about me. You know all that. I should go home to talk to them, like I promised I would."

"Now?"

"Yes, now. I never asked for any of this, and I can't take it anymore."

His heart stilled. "You can—"

"No! I don't want to hear that. I've had it. And don't tell me all that about God not giving us more than we can handle, because you're wrong. I know how much I can handle and this is way past that amount!"

"That's not true. You know—"

She brushed past him. "I know my limits, Eli. Look, my aunt wants me to come home. So I'm going."

"You didn't want to before."

"I never said that."

"If you'd wanted to go, you'd have packed up long ago, right?"

She sniffed. Even though she faced away from him, he knew she was struggling to hold back her emotions.

"You can't go. We're close to finding Noah. You owe that much to Trisha."

"We're no closer than we were a week ago. He's hiding somewhere nearby and nobody can find him. Not even you, and you claim to know him best! Look, Eli, you should just go down south, find Phoebe and talk to her. If anything, that'll lure Noah out of hiding." After rifling through the donated box, she threw the toiletries into the plastic bag from the deli. "And you won't have to worry about me. I'll be at home."

"And if Noah follows you? What do you think he'll do when he finds you living with people you love?"

She stopped her movements. "He won't do anything, because he won't find me."

"He had Trisha in his grasp for years! Don't you think he'd know where the rest of her family lived?"

"Nothing's going to happen!" She whirled around. "You just want me to stay because you're as controlling as your brother! And just as selfish! You want revenge because he took something you wanted to control, your own sister!"

He folded his arms. "And you're a Jonah."

"A what?"

"You're just like Jonah, the man from the Bible who ran away. He thought he knew what was right and that God was wrong, so he ran away from his responsibilities, just like you're doing."

He watched as red suffused her face. "Next thing you'll be saying is that I should trust God, that He knows best."

"You should." He took a step toward her.

She stepped backward. "And what about you? When was the last time you trusted God?"

He stilled. "I do trust Him."

"No, you don't. All I'm seeing is you desperate to find Phoebe and get your revenge on Noah for stealing her. So much so that you want to use me as bait!"

"That's not true." Even as the words tumbled from his lips, he knew they were a lie. He swallowed, hating himself and disturbed that Kaylee could so easily snap out the truth.

But was it still the truth? In the past week, he found himself caring more and more for her, until he reached the point he dared not cross. The point of admitting his feelings to her. A very dangerous point for both of them.

"It *is* true," she snapped back. "That's the only reason you don't want me to leave. You're not trusting God, either! Vengeance is mine, says the Lord, remember? So what are you doing? Getting back at Noah under the guise of freeing your sister! If you trusted God, you wouldn't be doing things that go against His teaching. So stop telling me what the Christian thing to do is, because you're not doing it, either!"

With that, she slapped down the bag.

Then she dropped into the chair beside the dresser.

Eli swallowed hard. Twice. *Lord, is what she saying true? I want to be in Your will, so help me, Lord.*

There was no wash of warmth, no comforting hand of God on his shoulder saying softly that what he was doing was right. God was as silent for him as He'd been for Kaylee. Eli just stared at her, until she looked up at him, her own stricken expression a mirror of his.

She was right. He was desperately trying to get back at Noah. How many times over the years had he considered hurting Noah, or worse?

"You're right," he finally whispered. "So right." He knelt down in front of her.

She held out her hands and he took them. "And so are you." Wetting her lips, she continued. "I *am* running away. I've always done it. The only time I didn't run from my problems, I tried to fix them by going to The Farm. I ended up held captive and fell under Noah's sway. Running away is usually easier for me, but in that compound, it was easier to stay. I was too scared to take any risks. But then when I did take one…"

"No," he said softly. He didn't want her to go through all that again. "You think that the Lord is punishing you for all the things you said, but part of it is humiliation, too."

She looked at him, obviously confused by his words. He explained himself. "You were humiliated by Noah. He not only tricked you with his blasphemy, but after he killed Trisha, he went the extra mile by claiming that he spurned your advances."

Tears slipped free of her eyes and flowed in two even tracks down her cheeks. They cut sharply into his heart. "Noah humiliated me, too, and I've been fighting back for years, trying to get even with him for it. He stole our sister and rubbed my nose in it."

She clung to his hands, then, a breath later, lifted them to her cheek. "We've run out of hope, haven't we?"

He brushed her cheek with the back of his hand, reveling in the peachlike feel of her skin and the warmth of her tears. "No. There's always hope."

"Lois told me that God promised us life more abundantly."

"And we've had that." He drew her hands closer to his chest, to keep at bay the temptation of holding her close, kissing her and starting something they shouldn't start. "Kaylee, sometimes God takes us to the absolute end so that He can show us He loves us and wants to help us. He takes us to the limit of our strength to show us His, so that we can finally admit that we need Him."

"And have you reached the end?"

He nodded. There was so much he wanted to say

to her, so much fear he'd felt himself, especially with her announcement that she was leaving. And just as importantly, he could now see the extent that the driven nature he despised in Noah was in him, too. Only one thing could help him conquer it.

A wealth of sudden insight bombarded him and he found himself searching for words, the words that could explain the thoughts racing through him.

"I've just realized everything, Kaylee. With your help. I've been trying to get revenge on Noah all these years. And you're right, I haven't trusted the Lord. I've been afraid I was like Noah, expecting that I would be like him and not really believing God could change me."

"We've both reached the end," she whispered, clinging to his hands. She shrugged, looking self-conscious. "Maybe I need Jesus in my life. I know that I can't go on by myself anymore."

He stared at her, too stunned to speak. Finally, he said, "You need Jesus, Kaylee, and He wants to be a part of your life."

The emotion of the moment overwhelmed him. He wasn't used to sharing his spirituality with anyone, let alone a woman he'd just met, tried to use and suddenly come to care very much for. He'd never before brought anyone to the Lord.

He dropped his head down, but she lifted it up, cradling it in her hands. "Pray for me, Eli. I think I need it."

His heart swelled, catching him in his throat and not letting go. "Oh, sweetheart, everyone needs prayer. Especially me right now."

"Then pray for both of us."

He prayed, his words so soft he wasn't sure Kaylee could hear them. But they weren't meant for her.

Kaylee was so right when she said he was after revenge. He prayed for guidance, wisdom, strength to do God's will. And he prayed for God to remove the vengeance in his heart, to change him.

When he lifted his head again, Kaylee was smiling. "Thank you."

He wanted to kiss her, to hold her and tell her every thought racing through him. But all he could do was stare at her.

She touched his cheek with her palm. "I don't think I could have done this without you. You have such strength and commitment and know what's right."

He laughed, a short one with a shake of his head. "You just told me I didn't trust God."

She turned sheepish. "I was mad because you were right about me."

"Just like you were right about me. I *have* been looking for revenge. But more than that, I've been scared."

"Of what?"

"Of turning out like Noah. Of being so driven that I don't know what God wants for me. And the more determined I got to stop Noah, the more I lost sight of what God wanted me to do. It wasn't until this moment that I could really see what He wants for me. He wants me to stop trying to do everything myself—and that includes getting revenge on Noah. He wants me to trust Him."

"You are trusting Him, just like I am now."

"It's more than that. I was using you and even though I knew it, I couldn't stop myself. And because

I felt I couldn't stop myself, I figured I was as bad as Noah. But all I needed to do was ask for help."

With that, he bowed his head.

His prayer was louder this time.

"Phoebe interpreted my fear as jealousy and selfishness. Maybe there was a bit of both there. I was really trying to keep myself from being like Noah, instead of letting the Spirit change me."

"There's so much I want to ask you about this."

He chuckled. "I feel like a bit of a novice, myself. But we'll find the answers together."

"Yes." On an impulse, she leaned forward and kissed him warmly on the lips. He returned it. And however brief their kiss, it touched his very soul.

Kaylee reached for a tissue and wiped her eyes before smiling at him again, relief pouring from her grin like water over Niagara Falls. "I just realized I still have to lock up the gym. Feel like driving me down there?"

"I'd love to."

They took their time leaving the motel, Kaylee pausing for a moment to fix his collar where she'd rumpled it. Then, they drove down to River Road.

The main street of the town had been temporarily repaired, thankfully, and they didn't have to detour. He swung the car in front of the line of stores, to park by the candy store.

She'd just given her life to Christ, he kept on thinking. It still stunned him. He'd been a committed Christian since he was a teenager. He'd seen this kind of thing before and yet, this time, it touched him so intensely.

He loved her. He truly loved her. He'd been walking

around the issue for days. It wasn't supposed to happen this fast. Love came after the long term, after a deep inspection of both souls.

And hadn't they just done that?

They walked past the candy store. Kaylee stopped, only feet from the front facade of the gym.

He looked down at her. She was staring at the side of the building. He followed her gaze. All he could see was the alley, and at the end of it, part of the unused shed at the back of the gym. Nothing unusual. "What's wrong?"

"Smell that?"

He sniffed. "Sweet-smelling. It's candy."

"Yes. They're made right there in the back of this store. They must have made some today."

Uneasy, he sniffed the air again. "What are you saying?"

She shook her head, before grabbing his hand and backtracking down the line of shops. At the end, they ducked into the next alley, only to come up behind the block.

He wanted to ask her what was going on, but she put her finger to her lips. They moved behind a medium-sized Dumpster. Ahead stood the back of the gym and, beyond, the playground and basketball courts.

"What are we doing here?" he asked softly.

She bit her lip. "I think I know where Noah's been hiding." She pointed down the alley.

He peered after her, not understanding. "Where?"

"The shed."

He looked down toward the right. The old shed stood with its back pressed into the forest. On the side closest to them was a narrow trail that led through the woods to the street across from Kaylee's cul-de-sac. He shook his head. "Tell me what you're thinking."

"The same thing you've been thinking all week. I've been smelling candy at the rec center. And when Noah showed up in my backyard, I smelled it again. But now they're making a new batch, so they couldn't have been making one this past week or earlier today. They don't sell that much."

"Maybe they're planning for the Christmas rush. It's only a couple of months away."

"No. You know what I mean. Jenn told me when I first came here that this business isn't that big. Besides, I've found the wrappers in the gym and down the hallway and outside the back of the building. I've been blaming the kids, but that candy isn't popular with them." She nodded toward the only door ahead of them, then fastened her gaze on him. "You've suspected he's been around here. Does Noah like candy, Eli?"

He nodded.

She turned toward the shed. "He's been hiding in there."

There was no point in denying that he'd considered what she'd just realized. "What's it used for?"

"I think it was originally meant for outdoor equipment, but the lock is no good and someone decided it wasn't big enough."

"Was the lock ever fixed?"

She lifted her shoulders briefly. "I don't think so. No money, I would say. There may not be anything in there now at all. But apart from the woods around here, where else could he be? He was handy when Hec

Haines saw him in the park and when we think about the incident with the dryer, it had to have been deliberate. I'm sure of it."

"Kaylee—"

"No, listen. Jenn said she pulled it out, but the cord is so long that you'd have to pull it out much farther to have the wires get ripped out. Even if the dryer had been vibrating, it was odd that it should choose that moment to short out." Her voice grew more excited. "And the candy wrappers. You said that Noah likes to toy with people. He did it with the candy. Jenn and I swept out behind the dryer and the wrappers were fresh. I could still smell the candy on them. And he was clean. He's been using the gym's facilities. He's somehow got a key and the alarm code and has been in every night. He moved the dryer memo, the dryer, the sandbags—"

"But why flood the gym?"

"Because I'm in charge of it. So I would get fired, be forced to move home—"

Eli held up his hand. "And become so despondent, you'd commit suicide." He sighed. "Yes, I suspected that he'd been coming into the rec center, but I didn't say anything."

"Why?"

"Because I didn't have proof and I didn't want you to take off before I could use you to lure him out." He looked sheepish. "I was selfish, remember?"

She touched his face. "And it's all forgiven now."

"But how's he getting into the rec center?"

"The same way he got into the shed. He picked the lock. Inside, he could easily find a spare key."

"He could be hiding in the woods. He took a survivalist's course once."

"But when I saw him, he looked clean and neat. He could have been cleaning up in the center at night. He'd have to in order to impersonate you."

Eli found himself frowning. Could Noah really be so close? Right under their noses all this time?

He stared at the storage shed. Kaylee had thought she'd seen Noah at the compound before it exploded. Was it possible that Noah was there, like she said?

Yes, it was possible. Noah was resourceful and he was also the type to take full advantage of a situation.

He liked to be comfortable, too.

And he had a sweet tooth.

He pointed to the door. "Does the door open inward or outward?"

Kaylee bit her lip and shook her head. "I don't know. The hinges are on the outside. I think it swings out."

"We need a plank of wood. Something to jam the door."

"We don't have anything like that here." She brightened suddenly. "We should call Officer Reading."

"And if Noah's not in there?"

She stiffened. "Look!"

Eli peered through the dusk. A sliver of dim light suddenly winked on under the door. It spread thinly out across the dark asphalt.

Someone was in the shed, all right. Instinctively, he drew her down in a crouch behind the Dumpster.

This was it. He drew out his cell phone and quickly tapped in the officer's number.

He explained the situation and Reading said he would be there within a few minutes.

Eli hung up. "He's on his way." He looked across

at the door, blowing out a sigh. "It's been seven years since I talked to Noah."

Kaylee touched his arm. "Remember your prayer."

Yes. He'd asked for God to wipe away the revenge in his heart, to give him the wisdom that he'd need to confront Noah after all this time.

Strength surged into him. "I remember. Yes, I can face him now." He turned to look into her face. "I would have killed him before, I was so angry at him. I'd have destroyed both our lives with my angry need for revenge."

She scanned his face, wonder in her expression. "Do you think there's a chance he'll see the truth, like what you've shown me tonight?"

"With God, all things are possible. Let's go."

"Go where?"

"I'm going to confront Noah now, before the police get here. I may never have the chance again."

Her smile faded. "Now?"

"Oh, sweetheart, it's okay. Trust the Lord."

TWENTY

Kaylee's heart pounded in her chest. *Lord, help us. Let us do the right thing here, for You.*

A peace settled over her, smoothly, like a warm comforter. Her heartbeat gently mellowed to a calming rhythm.

Yes, she could face Noah. He no longer had a hold on her. His threats were hollow, weak compared to the strength resonating in her.

She pressed her fingers into Eli's arm. "Okay, but first—this."

He looked down at her questioningly. She drew his face close to hers and touched his lips with hers, gently, gingerly.

Against her, he started slightly, causing her to smile as her lips brushed his. She'd caught him off guard.

But not for long. Eli wrapped his arms around her and pulled her close to return the kiss. Suddenly giddy, she tightened her own embrace and reveled in the delight his kiss gave her.

But they weren't huddled behind a Dumpster to share an intimate kiss. She drew back and, taking her cue, he set her away from him.

"Whew!" he said, breaking out into a wide grin. "You have quite a way of prepping a man for the biggest confrontation of his life. Now, where were we?"

She smiled. "Sorry about that. We were ready to face Noah."

He stood, bringing her up with him. "Never be sorry for kissing me like that, woman." He sobered. "Ready?"

"Yes, but shouldn't we wait until the police come? It'll only be a few minutes."

"No. I need to face him and so do you. There are some things I need to say to him before the police arrive. Like I said, trust the Lord."

They crept toward the shed. Reaching it, with its thin line of light at their feet, Eli grabbed the doorknob and pulled it open.

Noah spun around, surprise slapped on his face. He was crouched down over some cans, a section of metal pipe and other junk Kaylee didn't recognize encircling him. The room was strewn with candy wrappers and empty soda cans. In the far corner lay a rumpled, handmade quilt. She recognized it as one from her own house, donated by Lois. She shivered at the thought of how he'd stolen it.

Eli stepped ahead of her. "It's over, Noah."

She held her breath. Noah stood, slowly, his lips turning up in the same strange smile she'd seen on his face that evening in her backyard.

"Well, good for you, Eli, for finally putting everything together." As if to taunt him, he slowly unwrapped a candy and popped it into his mouth. "Looks like you're actually getting smart."

Beside her, she felt Eli stiffen. "Smarter and wiser

than you realize, Noah. This time, you're going to face the police and you won't be able to talk your way out of murder like before."

Noah flicked a glance in her direction. It barely landed on her before he discarded it, as if she meant nothing to him. "Murder? Whose murder?" he asked Eli.

"John's and, of course, Trisha's."

He laughed and flicked his head in her direction as he picked up some wires he'd dropped. "Is that what she told you? She's delusional. She doesn't even know what to believe herself."

"I do," she snapped back. "And I know that you'll never hurt me again."

"Really?" He tightened his grip on the wire in his hand.

Eli became a blur. He snatched Noah's wrist and dug his fingers into the soft flesh. Crying out, Noah crumpled in pain and released the length of wire he held. It dropped on top of the pipe and Jenn's missing scissors and various cans.

The same kinds of stuff she'd seen once in the basement of The Farm.

Suddenly, everything came clear for her. Time slowed for her. "Eli!" she cried. "Stop him! He's making a bomb!"

Eli then twisted his brother's arm to his back and forced him to the floor. Noah groaned as his face scraped the harsh, dirty cement.

"No more, Noah! Not one more blasted thing! It's over!"

Kaylee rushed forward. A fast prayer leaped into her brain. *Help Eli, please, Lord.*

Immediately, Eli eased up on his grip. Noah gasped and swore loudly, but remained firmly pinned to the floor.

Keeping Noah's arm in that painful, awkward position, Eli turned to her. "How did you know he was making a bomb?"

She gasped and glanced over the junk on the floor. "He was?"

"Yes. And I have a feeling he was reaching the most dangerous part." Eli dragged his brother to standing, and then out of the shed, forcing him to the dark, wet asphalt halfway up the alley. With a horrified look behind her, Kaylee followed them out.

"I suspected something was wrong, then you called out," he told her.

Kaylee backed away, taking small steps toward the candy store. "I shouted? I saw him moving his hand and just knew something was wrong. What did I say?"

"My name and something about a bomb. You don't remember?"

She shook her head.

Bright lights flooded into the narrow alley between the center and the candy store. They cut across Noah's face as Eli held him down. A moment later, Officer Reading trotted down toward them.

Eli grabbed his arm. "There's some explosives in that shed! You'll want to get the bomb squad in."

Reading gaped at them. "What? Get out of here! Nearest place you can be is the far end of the park, okay?"

"They're working in the candy store, too, tonight."

"I'll get them, don't worry." After speaking quickly into his shoulder mike, he pulled Noah up and stood him beside Eli. His head snapped back and forth. "Wow, you guys could be twins."

"No," Kaylee corrected, stepping closer, her heart racing from all that had happened. "Noah is thinner, weaker, paler."

Noah spat out something garbled. An obscenity, most likely. Eli's eyes narrowed and Kaylee could see he was looking at his brother through Kaylee's eyes, seeing him as she did. Thinner, weaker, paler.

"Enough!" Officer Reading smacked handcuffs on him and quickly patted him down to ensure he wasn't armed. "All right. You'll have plenty of time to talk later. Let's get out of here."

Kaylee watched him lead Noah down the alley. Noah stumbled, but being bigger and stronger, Reading hauled him up. Silhouetted against the bright alley spotlights at the end of the cruiser's light bar, the two men seemed to echo a feeling of total sadness.

She straightened just as Eli took her hand to hurry her down the alley. Incredible. She didn't feel any hatred toward Noah. None at all.

They reached Noah as Reading was preparing to shove him into the cruiser. Kaylee stepped past Eli to face him. "Your days of murder and robbery and trying to kill me are over."

Noah sneered. "And you think you're smart figuring it all out, I bet."

"You were at The Farm when it blew up, weren't you?"

"I knew it wouldn't be long before Eli conned you into coming. You're easy to manipulate."

She refused to rise to his insults. "And that's how

you managed to sneak into Canada. You followed the same route we took."

"It wasn't hard. You two were running for your lives making a trail as wide as a road."

"Why did you break into the center? To clean up?"

"Why not?" He shrugged. "I could keep up with your schedule, shower, shave..."

"Try to kill me!"

"I'd rather you'd been fired for letting the water in, losing things, leaving the place a mess." Noah laughed. "Then you'd be so depressed, you'd commit suicide."

"You mean you'd kill me."

"Your words, not mine."

Kaylee shook her head. "I figured that was your plan. But Jenn was more understanding than you thought. And so you decided to trip me and have me fall into that creek."

"It was swollen enough for you to drown, especially someone as weak as you."

"Too bad I have found new strength."

He leaned forward menacingly, his mouth twisting horribly. "You'll never find peace after what you did for me."

Eli cut between them. "You're wrong. And your power is gone. Your cult has fled and dispersed."

"Is that what you think? You don't even know where they've gone."

"Wrong. And I know how best to approach Phoebe," Eli answered. "It's time for the healing to begin, for all of them, starting with her."

Kaylee took his arm, but continued to stare at Noah. "Yes. And I'm ready to heal, too. You killed John, as well as Trisha. John would never blow himself up, not even for you. But you needed him to die so we'd stop looking for you. You rigged that explosive to go off early, didn't you?"

Noah turned away. "Pure speculation."

"No, it's not. I know you killed Trisha, but I'm ready to move past that, now."

He discarded her words with a belligerent tone. "Trisha killed herself."

She shivered and Eli drew her close. Reading took the cue to push Noah's head down as he climbed into the backseat of the cruiser. Sirens yowled in the distance. "Go over to the park, now," Reading yelled at them. "Now!"

After they'd crossed the street, Reading called out, "And stay there!" Then he hurried to the candy store.

Kaylee's attention strayed toward the car. Noah twisted around and, through the back windshield, smirked at her. In the yellow of the streetlights, he looked as he had behind her house. But the smirk had an intensity that made her shiver.

She shook her head, disgusted.

Abruptly, she stopped and straightened. She'd stood up and faced Noah, without a single ounce of fear in her.

Amazement flooded through her. "I did it! I faced Noah! With the Lord's help."

From behind, Eli wrapped his arms around her. "It's a great feeling, isn't it?"

Tears burned her eyes and she blinked several times to clear her vision. Eli's smiling face was close to her right. Her heart clenched as a word returned to her.

Itinerant. He was only here to find Noah, to stop

him so he could fulfill his ultimate goal of freeing Phoebe.

That was done.

The tears sprang back into her eyes and she sniffed.

"Don't."

Twisting around, she blinked Eli back into focus. "Don't what?"

"Don't cry. I know what you're thinking and it's not going to happen."

"You're going to leave, aren't you?"

"No!" He tightened his grip on her, yet shut his eyes and sighed. "I know. It's all I've wanted for the last seven years. It's finally coming true and I find myself not wanting to leave you. Because I love you. I love you more than I ever thought I could love another person."

She pulled back enough to see his face. "You love me?" A laugh spilled from her mouth. "I love you, too. I've pushed it away now for days, not wanting to deal with it. Like you said, I'm a Jonah. I knew you would leave eventually. I knew you'd be gone once you found Noah or learned where Phoebe was. And I didn't want to admit that I loved you if you were going to leave me."

He kissed her, then held her tight again. "I know how it feels. And I hate to think that I would ever leave you, even for a short time. But this is something I have to finish. I have to close this part of my life. I don't…"

"Take me with you, then. We'll find her together and we'll get the best people to help us approach her."

His eyes lit. Such beautiful blue eyes. "Are you sure? They may not be where we think they are. We may be chasing a wild goose. You need stability and you have a life here now."

"We'll be back. You need to do this and, in a way, so do I. I wouldn't have gone with you yesterday, but today, I can. I *want* to go. God is giving us this opportunity to help Phoebe and the rest of them. It's amazing how everything is turning out, isn't it?"

"We'll be back. I promise. We'll fly down as soon as possible, then we'll come back here." He lifted his eyebrows questioningly. "When we get back, will you marry me, Kaylee? Right here?"

She pulled his head toward hers, grinning widely. Joy rushed through her. "I'll marry you anywhere, but it would be extra special to marry you here."

Officer Reading had already reached them as they were finishing their kiss. "Are you two done?"

They split quickly.

With a hint of a smug smile, Reading continued, "I need you two down at the station. I have another patrol car on the way to take you."

Over his shoulder, Kaylee noticed the owners of the candy store hurrying away from the building, one of them throwing a curious look at the parked cruiser and at Noah.

Reading continued, "The bomb squad is on their way, too, but thankfully, from what I can see when I peeked in, something amazing has happened."

"What do you mean?" Kaylee asked.

"You two confronted Nash before we got there. Normally, it would be a stupid idea, but this time it saved our lives. If Nash had been given another few minutes, he'd have armed that explosive and in the next second, he'd have killed everyone around him."

Kaylee's knees weakened. Eli grabbed her and

kept her upright. A nauseous swell rolled through her stomach.

"But," Reading added, leaning toward Eli as a serious frown creased his forehead, "I don't ever want you to take the law into your own hands again. Do you hear me?"

"God was with us," Eli said softly.

Reading remained stern. "Yeah, but we're also told not to tempt Him. Let the police do their jobs next time."

"He will." Kaylee gripped Eli's arm. She wasn't about to let Eli play the superhero again.

They waited until the other police car arrived, which took them to the station. As they were leaving, Kaylee turned around to see if Reading's cruiser was following them, but it remained parked by the gym. She could see Noah's head bowed, his body slumped. From the back, he looked old and frail.

At the station, the other officer led them in. She stopped him. "I need to call my boss. She runs the gym. She should know what's happened."

"Give me her number and I'll call her."

Kaylee recited it, then the officer excused himself, leaving Eli and her alone in one of the small interrogation rooms.

The minutes ticked by. While she sat in one of the plastic chairs, Eli paced back and forth, his arms first crossed, then shoved deep into his pockets, then up to scrub his face.

"Eli?"

He stopped. "What's wrong?"

"You. You're wearing a rut in the floor. We're just here to give a statement. It's over." She stood and laid her hand on his shoulder, squeezing it and massaging it absently. "One thing that's good in all of this, is that Noah didn't die. He'll be able to stand trial."

He took her hand and squeezed it back. "What Noah did to our family made it personal to me and yet I handled it all without losing my cool."

"God intervened. Didn't you say something about Him taking us to the end to show us how much we need Him and how much He can minister to us and how much He really loves us?"

Eli smiled, but the expression held sadness. "That's good, sweetheart. But I'm realizing now that Noah made it even more personal when he tried to hurt you."

"It doesn't mean you don't love your family any less, if that's what you're thinking."

"For years I wanted to kill him."

"But you didn't."

"I wanted to and that's just as bad."

"And that's the great thing about Jesus, isn't it? He'll forgive us and we can start again." She cupped his jaw, tilting her head to stare into his eyes. "He forgave me and you should have heard the things I said and did."

He turned his face and kissed her palm. "You're good at witnessing, you know that?" He sighed. "And with Noah alive, he can't be turned into a martyr by his cult."

The door opened and in walked Reading. His face appeared pinched and dark. "I have some bad news. Something has happened to your brother."

Eli shifted Kaylee behind him. "What is it?"

"He was conscious and rather belligerent one moment, in the back of the cruiser and the next minute, he collapsed and lost consciousness. We called the paramedics. They rushed him to the hospital, with two other officers."

"How is he now?"

Reading shook his head. "He didn't regain consciousness. His heart just stopped and they couldn't revive him at the hospital. I'm sorry."

"He's killed himself?" Eli asked.

"We don't know that."

"Did the emergency-room doctor see any signs of poisoning? He was eating candy when we caught him."

"I don't have any details yet. The other officers haven't returned. There'll be an autopsy and an inquiry; you can count on it." He lifted his brows, looking grim. "But you're right. It does look like suicide. I remember thinking that he looked a weird shade of green. I've seen some drug overdoses before, but nothing like that."

Kaylee waited for the surge of some emotion. But all that came was a deep sadness. "He'll never stand trial for killing Trisha."

Eli turned to look at her. "He'll be judged eventually, as we all will."

She peered up at him, taking the step closer to allow him to draw her into his arms. "Still, I don't want Trisha to be remembered as the one who committed suicide. It's not simply a matter of justice. It's her memory I don't want to be tarnished."

Reading shook his head, his face full of determination. "There'll still be an investigation into her death, I promise you. I can't promise what the outcome will be, but I'll do my best to make sure you're heard."

Tears watered her eyes. "Thank you."

But she couldn't help but wonder how much they'd listen to her now, when they didn't listen before. With Noah dead and Phoebe still to be found, what proof did she have?

TWENTY-ONE

Tallahassee's brilliant sunshine blinded Eli. He and Kaylee had decided to fly down, and now, walking out of the airport with Roger, his investigator, he searched for his sunglasses. The moment he located them in his pocket, he fumbled and dropped them. Kaylee stooped to retrieve them.

"It's going to be all right," she whispered. "She's already been told of Noah's death. And it's had time to sink in. The only other women with her right now are Janice and Tina."

"Are you sure? The photo didn't show their faces."

"I know who they are by their shapes. It's good for us."

"Why?"

"Remember I told you about that woman who picked the lamb's-quarter? That was Janice. Noah punished her. I think she began to be disillusioned after that."

"And the other woman?"

"A couple of years ago, Tina became pregnant. She lost the baby. He was stillborn, poor thing. Tina nearly died herself. These two women weren't as adamant in following Noah after what happened to them. Not like some of the group."

"Like Phoebe?"

"I know what you're getting at. But Phoebe has also got the truth about Noah now staring her in the face. The police down here showed her a copy of the autopsy and the proof that he killed himself." She offered him an encouraging smile. "Have a little faith, okay?"

They had reached Roger's car. Across the trunk, Eli returned the smile. "Thanks. I wish we'd have checked Noah's mouth before he climbed into the cruiser."

"The candy was covered with the poison. He'd planned it. He must have had it in his pocket all week. And with all those wrappers around, we wouldn't have been surprised to see one shoved in his mouth. You couldn't have known he was prepared like that."

"No, but still—"

She plowed on. "He had enough poison in that shed to kill the entire cult. I thank God that he hadn't headed south with the rest of them. He could have killed them all."

Roger unlocked the passenger door for them. "You should be thankful he didn't try to poison either of you. He had plenty of opportunity. I have the exit counselor meeting us near the campground. She'll help you deal with this."

Kaylee watched Eli nod in gratitude. The drive into the campground was long and they had to pick up the exit counselor halfway there. In the quiet of the backseat, she watched Eli drop his head and close his eyes.

He was praying.

Lord, listen to his prayers. Give him the right words. All for Your glory, Lord.

After they registered and drove into the small tent and trailer park, she caught Eli's eyes.

He swallowed. She repeated her prayer. Roger consulted the campground map and turned left into the tenting area. Huge oak trees, so different than the ones she'd grown up with, along with slender palms, graced the grounds, giving the area an exotic Edenlike feel.

Roger stopped the car at one of the empty campsites. Everyone climbed out. Immediately, Eli's gaze, followed by hers, fell on a small dome tent across the road. A woman emerged from it.

Phoebe. Kaylee froze and so did Eli.

"Phoebe?" Both she and Eli spoke at the same time.

Kaylee stepped forward, past the car, toward the young blond woman. "It's Eli. He's here to talk to you."

Dazed, Phoebe tore her gaze from Kaylee to Eli and back again. "I know. I just didn't expect him to look so much like Noah used to look. It's…it's been so long."

Then she broke down. Within milliseconds, Eli was there, holding his little sister close. Kaylee watched with watering eyes as Phoebe clung to her brother.

"I'm sorry," the younger woman sobbed. "I'm so sorry!"

For several long minutes, Kaylee, the investigator and the exit counselor watched and let the siblings begin their healing.

Finally, they broke their embrace. Eli led her to the picnic table. Kaylee took a step toward them, but the exit counselor caught her arm.

"Why don't we go for a walk for a few minutes?"

Reluctantly, Kaylee allowed the woman to lead her

away. She wanted to be by Eli's side, to hold on to him, to give him the security and the prayers he'd given her. But this was something just for the siblings.

The fifteen minutes they took wandering around the campground felt like years. When they finally returned to Phoebe's site, the siblings were hugging again. The exit counselor cleared her throat.

Wiping her eyes, Phoebe approached Kaylee. "And I'm so sorry for what has happened to you. For what I did to you."

Kaylee blinked, confused by her words. "What did you do to me?" She was half afraid of the answer.

Phoebe hugged herself. Her eyes were rimmed with red. "I was the one who told the police those lies about you, when Trisha died."

The world around her seemed to spin. "You said what?"

Phoebe's small mouth twisted and her chin wrinkled. "I can't believe I lied for Noah. I told the police you were angry and had left because he'd spurned you. I told them Trisha became so upset that she threatened to kill herself more than once." Tears spilled down her cheeks. "I'm so sorry. It wasn't until Janice brought me here and we heard about Noah that I realized how awful I'd been." Her voice wobbled. "How awful we all were, all in the name of something terribly wrong. I actually thought it was for the greater good to lie and keep the world away from us. But we were just hiding our heads in the sand like ostriches."

Sympathy washed over Kaylee. Gone was the anger, the hatred. They'd all been victims. "I know how you feel. But it feels so much better to face your fears."

Phoebe hiccuped a small sob. "I was afraid. Noah

had given us such a horrible picture of the outside world, that I was scared to go anywhere. But being here, I see it's not so bad."

Kaylee pulled Phoebe into a warm, forgiving hug. The young girl clung to her, whispering an apology over and over.

The exit counselor stepped up and touched both women's shoulders. They moved apart. "This is where I step in." She led Phoebe away. Kaylee watched them, feeling Eli walk up behind her and wrap his arms around her waist.

"I love you," he whispered in her ear. "And I'm so proud of you. You've done the right thing here. Not too many people do that."

She clung to his arms. "Not too many people have what I have. A Savior and a wonderful fiancé."

"Who both love you very much."

Dear Reader,

Has one story ever inspired you? Touched you? Did the story have so many layers that each time you studied it, you found more to ponder? They're the signs of a great work. One story, The Book of Jonah, touched me like that and inspired me to write *Desperate Rescue.*

Kaylee in this story is on the run from God. She thinks she knows better than He does and rebelliously fights every attempt God makes to reach her.

Perhaps there is a piece of Jonah in all of us, that touch of rebellion against God, when we think we know what's best for ourselves. And sometimes it takes the very bottom, the end of the road, to make us reach out and ask for help.

Even the most humble, the most unassuming person, such as the introverted Kaylee, has a streak of rebellion in them, but the good news is that all we have to do is ask God for help and He delivers.

Ask for help. Try it. Suggest it to your loved ones when they're struggling. Tell them to read Jonah and give them this book. If Jonah could pray from the belly of a whale, we can pray anywhere or anytime.

God Bless,

Barbara Phinney

QUESTIONS FOR DISCUSSION

1. In a few short words, how would you describe Kaylee at the beginning of the book? Eli? And at the end of the story? How do the descriptions contrast?

2. Eli knew what would happen if Kaylee saw him and he asked her to return to the cult, but he did it anyway. Why? Would you do the same thing if you were desperate enough? What could Eli have done differently? Would it have been as effective?

3. Kaylee had some basic Christian knowledge at the beginning of the story, but it was distorted by Noah Nash's warped philosophies. Do you think she would have continued to go to church if Eli hadn't shown up? Do you think the others in the community could have helped her heal? Would you be as susceptible as Kaylee was under the same circumstances?

4. Kaylee believed she needed time to heal before she returned to any church. Do you agree? Do you believe that it's important to replace wrong thinking with right thinking immediately? Read Luke 11. What do you think was the real issue here?

5. God worked in both Eli and Kaylee's lives. Did you see definite examples of His presence? Name them.

6. Eli calls Kaylee a Jonah. Do you agree with him? How was Kaylee similar to Jonah? How was she different?

7. At the climax of the story, Eli decides to confront his brother. How do you think this decision came about? Do you think it was wise?

8. At what point do you think Kaylee decides to give God a chance? At the time she asks Jesus into her heart? Or was it before that? Why do you think she made this decision?

9. Kaylee faces Phoebe at the end of the story. What taught her to forgive the woman? What risks did she take when she faced Phoebe? What risks did she take when she faced Noah?

10. We all have people in our lives that we find hard to forgive. What could you do to help you learn to forgive those in your life who have hurt you?

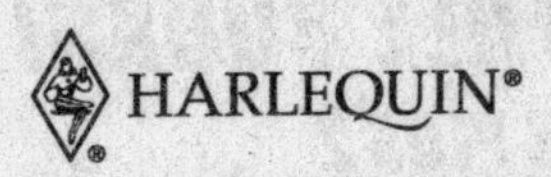

American ROMANCE®

COMING NEXT MONTH

#1149 THE DOCTOR'S LITTLE SECRET by Jacqueline Diamond
Fatherhood
Dr. Russ McKenzie doesn't have much in common with shoot-from-the-hip policewoman Rachel Byers. Nevertheless, he shares his little secret with her. Soon the two of them could be keeping it for life!

#1150 HER PERFECT HERO by Kara Lennox
Firehouse 59
The firefighters of Firehouse 59 are stunned when Julie Polk decides to convert a local hangout into a *tearoom!* Determined not to let that happen, they elect resident Casanova Tony Veracruz to sweet-talk the blonde into changing her mind. But when Tony wants more than just a fling with Julie, he's not sure where his loyalties lie....

#1151 ONCE A COWBOY by Linda Warren
Brodie Hayes is a former rodeo star, now a rancher—a cowboy through and through. Yet when he finds out some shocking news about the circumstances of his birth, he begins to question his identity. Luckily, private investigator Alexandra Donovan is there to help him find the truth—but will it really change who he is?

#1152 THE SHERIFF'S SECOND CHANCE by Leandra Logan
When Ethan Taggert, sheriff of Maple Junction, Wisconsin, hears Kelsey Graham is coming home for the first time in ten years, he wants to be there when she arrives. Not only is he eagerly anticipating seeing his former crush, he's also there to protect her. After all, there's a reason she couldn't return home before now....

www.eHarlequin.com

HARCNM0107